SAP RISING

SAP RISING

Christine Lincoln

PANTHEON BOOKS, NEW YORK

All rights reserved under International and Pan-American Copyright
Conventions. Published in the United States by Pantheon Books, a
division of Random House, Inc., New York, and simultaneously in
Canada by Random House of Canada Limited, Toronto.

Pantheon Books and colophon are registered
trademarks of Random House, Inc.

Library of Congress Cataloging-in-Publication Data
Lincoln, Christine.
Sap rising / Christine Lincoln.
p. cm.
ISBN 0-375-42140-8
1. United States—Social life and customs—20th century—
Fiction. 2. African Americans—Fiction. 3. Rural
conditions—Fiction. I. Title.

PS3612.I53 S27 2001   813'.6—dc21   2001021959

www.pantheonbooks.com

Book design by Johanna S. Roebas

Printed in the United States of America

First Edition

2   4   6   8   9   7   5   3   1

FOR ROBERTA LINCOLN

The ancient people perceived the world and themselves within that world as part of an ancient continuous story comprised of innumerable bundles of other stories.

LESLIE MARMON SILKO

Therefore I have declared that which I did not understand. Things too wonderful for me, which I did not know; hear now, and I will speak.

JOB

Contents

Bug Juice   3

A Hook Will Sometimes Keep You   20

Acorn Pipes   31

All That's Left   46

More Like Us   60

Sap Rising   65

Winter's Wheat   72

Wishes   92

Last Will   103

A Very Close Conspiracy   120

At the Water's End   139

Like Dove Wings   152

SAP RISING

BUG JUICE

She came into Sonny's life like wind, like a storm that blew in one night and was gone the next, leaving him with a yearning that would take years to fill. At first Sonny thought he was still caught in the depths of his dream, but then a stronger force pulled him back to a moon-soaked room, and into the lingering laughter that filtered through the cracks in his bedroom door and sounded like stars. Sonny knew the sounds of night surrounded by the softness of Moss Woods. For nine years he'd slept in that room, with the worn mahogany bureau, the paneled wardrobe, and the cedar chest, listening to his younger brother's and parents' breathing against the monotonous drone of insects and frogs spirited under the cover of darkness.

Sonny swung his legs over the side of the bed. He had gone to sleep in nothing but his underwear. And as he stood up, stretching his slight frame, a hint of the muscles that would pull him into manhood seemed somehow clearer in the moon's light. He picked his way to the door, opened it a crack, and slid through, pulling it quickly behind him as he went to stand at the top of the stairs. The glow from the kitchen cast the stairway into shadows, so Sonny had to hold on to the banister as he made his way to the bottom step. He could make out the voices of his mother and father and of another man whose voice he did not know. He poked his head around the corner, blinking his watery eyes against the kitchen's sudden brightness.

His father sat at the head of the table, his mother at the other end, her back to Sonny. A man sitting to the right of his mother poured himself a glass of beer from the paper bag he held in his hand. The man was around his parents' age, Sonny could see that. He was a shade lighter than his drink, with a sprinkling of freckles across the bridge of his nose and eyes that smiled even as his mouth disappeared behind his glass. A woman sat beside him, and once Sonny had seen her, he could not take his eyes from her. She was the darkest person he had ever seen, with almost everyone in his family being light-skinned and freckled.

But this woman was the color of ripened mulberries, the purple-black stain that covered Sonny's lips and hands when he gorged himself on the fruit's sweetness. Her cheekbones were so high the lower portion of her face seemed to belong to someone else. She sat quiet, looking back and forth among the other three as they traded conversation. Sonny shifted his weight, and the movement caught his father's eyes.

"What're you doin' up this time of night? You supposed to be sleepin'."

His mother turned around in her chair, her face a picture of pursed lips and contorted eyebrows as she tried to capture Sonny's eyes with her own. Before Sonny could come up with an excuse that would satisfy her, the beer man said, "Sonny! That you? My Lord, you done got big since the last time I saw you. Tall."

Sonny smiled, tucking his chin into his chest.

"You know who I am?" He didn't wait for Sonny to reply. "I'm your uncle Kenny. Remember me?"

Sonny's smile spread into a grin. He nodded his head hard so that it felt as if it would fall off and roll across the kitchen floor.

"Come over here. Let me get a good look at you." His uncle Kenny stretched his arms toward him, and Sonny flew from his mother's accusing eye and into the welcomed embrace.

Sonny felt himself engulfed in a close, quick hug before being taken by the shoulders and held at arms' length. His uncle's eyes searched Sonny's flushed face until he seemed satisfied with what he read there.

"You got yourself a fine young man here, Leonard, Sissy. Looks like Daddy when he was a boy, don't he?" His uncle turned to the woman by his side. The palm of his hand lay against the back of Sonny's neck, and Sonny was sure his uncle would be able to feel the heat rise up in his body. "Annie, this is Sissy's oldest boy, Sonny."

Sonny could feel the woman looking him over. He wanted to look at her, too, but didn't. She was from the city, and his mother had told him about city folks. How they was evil, devils, all of them going to hell except Uncle Kenny, who still had a chance at salvation since he hadn't actually been born there.

"Yes," his mother said. "This one here's a good one, as long as I stay on him. You gots to stay on chirrun these days—"

"And what about that other one?" His uncle Kenny squeezed Sonny's neck.

"Now, that Dennis, he's somethin' else, child."

"He was, what? three, four when I was last here?"

"Three. Just turned seven." Sonny could feel himself disappear once his mother's words were off him. "And when I say he's a mess, I mean he is just a *mess*. 'Bout a week or so ago, I come outside, and the boy had let all the chickens out of the coop. He running behind, talkin' about, 'Fly away, birds, fly away. You free!' "

"Lord have mercy!" Sonny's uncle sputtered, choking on a sip of beer. Everyone at the table laughed, as Sonny slipped away to go sit in the corner of the room. The conversation flowed around him like sea currents, and he was relieved that his uncle had diverted his mother's attention. He watched the way Annie nodded her head at the stories shared, laughing at the parts she was supposed to. Every now and again she would say something to his mother in a voice that sounded like dusk.

She didn't look like she was evil, with her soft hazel eyes

6

and a laugh that pulled him to the edge of his seat. Sonny watched as a moth fluttered against the screen door, trying to get to the light over the porch. The hum of insect wings and the drone of the conversation weighted his eyes, and his lashes began fluttering against the top of his cheeks. When he heard his name he nearly jumped from his seat, eyes wide and blind at the sound of his mother's voice.

"Come on, little boy. It's time for you to get back to bed."

"But I ain't tired." He tried to keep his voice from a whine. Sonny hated it when his mother called him a little boy, as if he were a child like Dennis. "Besides, it's too hot."

He crossed his arms over his chest, imagining he had become one with the chair. His mother crossed her arms as well, and Sonny could see that she was going to push the issue, even in front of this Annie woman.

"Let the boy go, Ruthie," Sonny's father said.

"Leonard, he needs to get his butt in the bed."

"How 'bout he come sit out on the porch with me?" Annie said.

Sonny's mother turned to the woman at her brother's side. She tilted her head, her eyebrows arching into her hairline as she looked down the length of her nose at the other woman.

"I mean, if that's OK with you all?"

Sonny's mother said nothing at first, just continued to look at the woman. She waited. Sonny knew she was good at that. Could ride the space between the passing of time and the beat of a person's heart for just that right moment. As if she knew just how long it took to let a person know everything he or she needed to know.

"I guess it's all right. But——" His mother raised her finger as Sonny bounded out of his chair. "But you not goin' to be out there that long. So don't get yourself too comfortable."

"Yes, ma'am."

Sonny walked across the kitchen and past his mother, his steps slow and measured. His knees quivered like a colt's from the strain of trying to keep himself from running as he made his way out the door and onto the porch with Annie.

"Let's go sit on the steps, Sonny," she said once they were outside.

Sonny went over to the screen and pushed at the heat-swollen wood until the door gave way and opened into blackness. He and the woman sat down on the cement steps. It was cooler out here, much cooler than inside, making the boy suddenly aware of his bare skin.

"It's beautiful here," she whispered.

Sonny looked around the blackened yard, his face a puzzle. "Don't you have nuthin' like this where you from?"

"Not in the city."

She pointed to the heavens. "See how big the sky is?"

Sonny followed her finger. The sky looked the same as it always did.

"It ain't so big where I live."

"You mean it's smaller? The sky?"

"Oh, yes, much smaller. Folks made it that way."

"Folks can make the sky shrink?" The boy cut his eyes at the woman.

"In the city they can."

Sonny leaned against the stair. His mama might be right, he thought. Maybe those folks *is* devils, anytime they can take

God's Heaven and make it smaller, and he told her he believed it's cause everyone there's going to hell anyway.

"They don't need such a big Heaven nohow," he said.

Her laugh surprised him, filling the air with the sound of
wind chimes. Made him smile, too.

"Sonny! Where you hear that from?"

"It's true, Miss Annie."

"Just Annie. And it ain't true. Look at me." She turned
around so the two of them faced each other. "You think I'm
goin' to hell?"

Sonny moved his eyes over the white teeth that gleamed in
the meager light, the softness in her face, and the eyes that
grinned at him. She didn't look like she was going to hell, and
even if she was, Sonny didn't care anymore.

"Naw," he said. "You don't appear to be no devil."

She threw back her head and laughed again, louder this
time. "You are a wise man, Sonny. How old are you, anyway?"

"Nine and three quarters."

"Yep, almost a man," she mused.

Sonny stuck his chest out and pulled back his shoulders.
He *was* almost a man. Though no one knew it except him and
now her. His mother sure didn't know. She treated him like
he was still Dennis's age. Probably hadn't even noticed how
he no longer played make-pretend games anymore. Or the
way his body had started to change.

Sonny inched himself closer to the woman by his side,
breathing deeply from the scent of her. She smelled like
some wild thing, like the deer his father sometimes shot and

hung in the barn to drain. Like yeast and dirt and summer storms.

"Look at 'em, the stars. Beautiful," she whispered. "These are the same stars that shine over Africa."

She pronounced it *Af-free-ka,* said she would go there someday before she died. That she would find the people who looked like her. Plum-black and beautiful, Sonny thought. She said there were whole tribes of people whose faces reflected her own, tribes where everyone was family. And Sonny could almost see the red-clay earth, the verdant hills, the rows of women wrapped in prisms of color, baskets on their heads, a swan's grace dance to the Nile. He blinked until he was looking at the row of trees that lined the edge of their land. They seemed taller somehow, majestic and proud. Sonny had never thought about a place on the other side of the ocean, only this place here.

"How you know all this? You a teacher?"

"Naw, I'm a . . . I dance." She looked at him. "But I read. Read all the time, everything I can get my hands on. Ask your uncle. He'll tell you. I read books by colored people, too."

Sonny sat up so that he could see her face. "You trying to make a fool outta me? Books by colored people?"

"Naw, I ain't making no fool outta you. It's true. Coloreds write books. They sure do."

Sonny wondered if his mother knew. The only book they owned was a Bible, and it was so old the cover had tore off a long time ago. Sometimes they listened to radio shows, but it was his mother who told him the stories as they sat on the porch each night, ones her mother had told her when she was a girl. He wondered if any of those stories had been written by a black man.

"What school you go to anyway, boy, that you don't know about Africa and colored writers?"

"We go to Hampton Elementary. It's been deseparated, you know. We with white folks now. But the year after next I'll be going to the junior high."

"Well, we gonna have to see that you get some real learnin'."

"Yes, ma'am." He looked back out at the trees. "Know what, Miss Annie?"

"What?"

"Nobody ever told me there was so many white people in the world." He looked at her to see if she would laugh. "I mean, I seen a few—Mr. Thom who owns the shoe store we go to, and the ones who come round on the weekends to sell wares. One even came and sat on this porch before. But I never knew until they sent me to that school it was so many of them and so few of us."

"I know, Sonny."

"And I never knew they hated me so much."

"Oh, Sonny." Annie placed her cool hand on the side of his heated face for the briefest of moments. The two fell silent. Just the crickets and her presence making the night alive.

Sonny let himself lean into her, resting his head on her shoulder. He could feel the rise and fall of her chest, every breath, every sigh that left her body, a shudder in his own. When she finally spoke, Sonny could hear the words gathering their strength from within her, as if from a well.

"There's this one story, it's called the story of the Sacred Tree of Life. It's a story about the self-created."

She took a deep breath before telling him a tale as ancient as river time. A time before Sun, Moon, and Earth. Where nothing existed except nothingness. That is, until the living spark that grew into flame, the fated battle between fire and cold, and the first goddess, Great Mother Ma—an African woman the color of dark fruit with cheekbones that looked as if they had been carved, Sonny imagined.

Sonny watched Annie's soft, full lips form words that fell around him in a hush before gathering strength. Her eyes, darker now, looked past him, through him, the light from the kitchen making them shine with the promise of the mysteries he felt.

She told him about the beauty of the Sun, Moon, and stars, a beauty created only after the most intense pain. How Great Mother Ma was struck in the back of the head so that she thought she would die, the essence of the pain falling from her lips in the shape of a brilliant, silvery orb to lodge itself in the heavens and from that day forth becoming the Moon. A terrible beauty. The origin of the hideous and the exquisite, one and the same. And Sonny could feel the spell tighten around him.

He could hardly stand the hearing of it, even if he didn't understand what all was meant. It was as if he stood at the edge of a precipice whose bottom he could not see. Her words were a murmur of streams that gathered into a mighty river and threatened to sweep him away.

"Sonny!" his mother yelled from inside.

He jumped at the sound of her voice. "Yes, ma'am?"

"It's time. We goin' on up."

"Comin'." Sonny got up from the step. "I gotta go, but I'll see you in the mornin'."

"I'll finish the story tomorrow night, OK?"

"All right."

"Then good night, Sonny."

"Good night, Annie."

Sonny walked into the kitchen, his mind filled with poisonous snakes that grew from the roots of the great tree and stars that came from a woman's fingertips. His uncle had already left the room. His mother's and father's backs disappeared around the side of the staircase. Sonny went up to his room knowing he would never be able to get back to sleep. He leaned his shoulder against his bedroom door, pushed it open, and stuck his head inside. Dennis had turned over onto his stomach, but his breathing was even and deep. Sonny slipped into the room and shut the door.

He waited for his eyes to get used to the natural light of the moon before going over to his bed. He could hear the creaking of his parents' bed as they settled in for the night. And when he could no longer distinguish the hush of their voices, Sonny knew they were finally sleeping. He wondered if Annie was still outside on the porch and decided that he would count to one hundred before going back downstairs to see.

The sunlight spread across Sonny's chest and face; he could feel it changing the color behind his drawn lids from black to red. It awakened him from a sleep absent of dreams and made him realize that he had somehow slumbered during the night.

He rolled over so he could see his brother's side of the room. Dennis was gone. Their mother had already been in to straighten his bed.

Sonny got up, grabbed his shorts and T-shirt from the floor, and put them on. With nothing else in his head except getting down to that kitchen, he bounded down the stairs with his legs splayed wide, one hand against the wall, the other on the banister. He rushed into the room only to find his mother standing alone.

"Set the table," she said without turning around.

"Yes, ma'am."

Sonny went over to the cabinet. He loaded his arms with plates to take to the table.

"Where's Daddy and Dennis?"

"He took Dennis to get his hair cut. They been gone since early. It's eleven o'clock."

"And Uncle Kenny?" he asked casually. He walked around the table, setting a plate in front of each chair.

"Still sleepin'. But he better get his butt up real soon. Him and that woman."

Sonny finished with the plates and went to get the silverware. When Annie entered the kitchen, she looked smaller than she had the night before. There was a puffiness around her eyes, a tiredness that no amount of sleep could erase. But as she stood with her back to the window, the sunlight framing her, Sonny didn't have to look hard to see the one who had sat with him beneath the stars and talked about a place called Africa.

"Mornin', Sonny, Sissy."

Sonny's mother turned to face her and said, "It's Ruthie."

"Oh, I'm sorry. I'm so used to Kenny calling you Sissy, I figured—"

"That's family."

Annie took a seat at the table as Sonny finished laying the rest of the forks and knives. He looked at her sitting hunched in her seat, like a child.

"In Africa, everyone's family. The whole tribe," Sonny said.

"Well, this ain't Africa," his mother snapped.

Sonny went to get the cups and saucers.

"Mama, did you know that they was black folks who wrote books?" He looked at Annie and smiled.

"Books?"

"Yes, ma'am."

"The only book you need to worry about is the Good Book, and you better not let nobody talk you into believin' nuthin' else. Now go wash your hands."

"Yes, Mama."

By the time Sonny came back into the kitchen, his mother had joined Annie at the table. He sat down in one of the chairs closest to Annie and looked back and forth between the two women. There was a tightness around the edges of his mother's eyes that had not been there before he left. Her lips were pursed almost flat. Annie just looked worn, tired.

The air between them trembled as if the last notes of a song had been played. Sonny began to eat the food his mother had already put on his plate.

"Brother needs to get up," his mother said. "I have to strip that bed so's I can wash those sheets. Just filthy."

Sonny frowned at his mother. "It ain't your laundry day."

"Don't be tellin' me what day it is, boy. I know what day it is. Besides, I'm sure they need washin'."

"Wha, the sheets?" Sonny stared at his mother, watched as her face blushed red. "Or Uncle Kenny and Annie?"

"Sonny Fisher!" his mother exclaimed.

Annie hid her mouth behind her napkin.

"Boy, what done got into you?"

"But Mama, you bein' rude."

"Who you think you are?" His mother's eyes widened with surprise and hurt.

Annie, who had been sitting quietly all this time, interrupted. "Sonny, you ought to apologize to your mother."

"Annie, I thank you, but I can handle my child," his mother said. "You." She pointed her finger in Sonny's face. "You wait until your father gets back here."

Annie finished her breakfast in silence before pushing herself away from the table. "Thank you, Ruth. Breakfast was real good. Now I think I'll go wake Kenny and see about us going." She looked at Ruth. "Don't want to overstay our welcome." And she got up and left the room.

"I thought they was stayin' until tomorrow?"

Sonny's mother avoided his eyes. "Changed their minds, I guess." She sighed, leaning back in her chair. "They was gonna leave anyways."

"Well, you sure didn't make her welcome," Sonny mumbled.

"And rightly so. And rightly so."

Sonny finished eating and went out to sit on the porch steps. He was still there when his uncle Kenny and Annie came outside to get in their car. The two stopped long enough for Kenny to flick a quarter into his empty hand and Annie to smile and brush the feather touch of her lips against his cheek. They promised him they would be back by evening. To say goodbye? Sonny would wait for her.

He stayed on the porch until his father and brother came home. His brother ran right off with his glove and ball for a neighborhood game like he and Sonny usually did every Saturday afternoon, while their father went into the kitchen for his breakfast. Sonny waited. He could hear his parents talking in a steady murmur broken every so often by his mother's exclamations.

"Sonny!" his father yelled from the kitchen.

"Yes, sir?"

"Come on in here, boy."

"Comin', sir."

Sonny walked into the kitchen, and his father pointed his fork at the chair to his left. "Have a seat."

Sonny sat down.

"Your mama told me you been sassin' her."

"Yes, sir."

"Well?"

Sonny looked over at his mother, who stood by the kitchen sink, her hands on her hips, watching him. "Sorry, Mama," he mumbled, more into his shirt than to his mother.

"*Humph.* You think you grown," she grumbled. She turned back to the sinkful of dirty dishes. "I know one thing."

"Ruthie, the boy's sorry."

"I ain't havin' no child of mine sass me in my own house. That's all I have to say."

Sonny looked at his father, who had started eating. They both knew that when she started in like this, only the spending of her energy could get her to stop.

"It's her, that's what. Comin' in here stirrin' things up. I say good riddance."

"They gone?" Sonny's father inquired.

"Not before Brother could take me for some money," his mother said.

"Won't see him for another hundred years."

"That's not true!" Sonny tried to keep his voice steady. "They comin' back to say good-bye to me."

"Oh, Sonny." His mother turned around to look at him, her eyes suddenly soft and warm.

"Don't look at me like that. It's true."

Sonny saw the look his mother gave her husband. "Daddy, can I be excused?" he asked.

"Yes, Sonny."

He got up from the table, his back ramrod straight, his chin quivering but lifted as if in salute. He climbed the stairs up to his room. She would come back. She would come back and finish her story. And he would leave with them. She had wanted to take him with her; he felt sure of that as he threw himself on the bottom of his bed, his face peering through the screen at the window. She would be his mother, teaching him things he would never learn if he stayed here, things he needed to know. Annie would tell him all about Africa, and they would go there together one day.

He stayed close to home all that afternoon. At times, he wandered down to the first floor and back up to the second as if lost. When dusk fell and his parents went out to sit on the porch while Dennis chased uncertain shimmers of fireflies in the increasing darkness, Sonny joined them. He moved past his mother and father as they sat on folding chairs and went to sit in the doorway with his back against the wood frame. The first eager stars made their presence known, and it was then, with his face to the heavens, that Sonny knew.

He could hear his parents talking in their low, steady tones, comforting the sadness that seemed to settle in his throat and push against the back of his burning eyes. Sonny looked over at the trees that lined the edge of their land. They were just trees—maple, cherry, apple.

"Hey, Sonny." Dennis ran across the yard toward him. "Come catch fireflies with me."

"Naw."

"Ah, come on. We can make jewelry."

Sonny remembered one of the stories his mother used to tell. The one that said how lightning bugs were beacons of light that guided lost souls home.

"It's just bug juice, Dennis," he said. "That's all."

A HOOK WILL
SOMETIMES KEEP YOU

Right there, I thought. That thing. I used to be so afraid of it.

It wasn't so much the rusted water pump, with the handle you had to work until air and then water gushed from its spout, but the well, the hole underneath, had terrified me. I use to believe I could just slip through the cracks between the wood planks and be gone.

I pulled the wagon with my son inside over to the patch of ragged grass in the center of the driveway and sat down beside the oak.

"Lord, this tree," I said out loud.

I don't know exactly when I first came here to live. It seems like always. But in the beginning, Aunt Loretta never let me forget that I hadn't been born at this place. I don't remember her, my mother. What she looked like, smelled like, tasted like. I was two when she left. But when I figured out she wasn't coming back, that was when I first became invisible. It was that birthday party that did it, my seventh. Before then, each year had come and gone with no more than a "Happy birthday" from Aunt Loretta, and a yearning for the woman I still called Momma.

But when I turned seven, Aunt Loretta gave me the most elaborate party, with balloons and games, cake and home-made strawberry ice cream. All the children came: Junie, Sonny, Cin, just everybody. We ran around the yard, around this tree, playing its and freeze tag. Wasn't until later, when everyone had gone home and the streamers lay crumbled in the grass and the balloons had been popped and small pink mountains of ice cream lay melting in the dirt, that I felt it. I knew she wasn't coming back, and it was at that moment a heaviness came over me. Started at my bare feet. Most folks think when you turn invisible you get lighter, but just the opposite is true. It's more of a leadening, as if you're being pulled into the earth. I felt tired, and when I looked down, I could see my feet fading into the grass and air.

I called out to Aunt Loretta, who came running out of the house. When she got to where I was sitting on the bottom porch step, all I could do was point at my dust-covered toes. "Look," I screamed. "Look at my feet, Aunt Loretta."

She couldn't see it, couldn't see nothing. Lord, I was frantic, jumping up and down and pointing all the while at my feet. "I'm turning invisible, I'm dissedappearing, Auntie."

"Pontella, you cut this foolishness out, you hear me?" she said in a trembling voice.

"Help me, Auntie," I cried, falling down into her lap. I cried until all I had left was the hiccups inside my chest. My eyes were puffed, near swollen shut. But when I looked down at my feet, my legs had faded up to my knees.

With a scream, I jumped up from Aunt Loretta and ran over to this tree, then scrambled up its limbs so quick she didn't have time to stop me. When I was younger, I would always climb this tree, to sit in the crook of its branches and let the breezes rock me. Made me think this must have been what it felt like when I was a baby. Like being held in my momma's arms.

Aunt Loretta begged me to come down. She stood at the base of the tree wringing her hands, twisting the bottom of her floral dress, stroking the fabric with her thumbs, pleading with me. But I refused. It was as if the tree, the solid roughness beneath my fingers, was the only thing that could keep me. I stayed there all the rest of that day, into the evening. Aunt Loretta stayed with me; she sat down at the foot of the tree listening to my sobs until night, when I lowered myself from the oak and let her take me into the house. She tried to get me to eat, but I was too tired. Instead I fell across my bed, and before I could even get my head down good on the pillow, I was fast asleep.

The next morning, the first thing I did was look down at my legs. I was still gone, now up to my thighs. I ran from the house and up into the tree. Aunt Loretta, who was in the kitchen frying slabs of bacon for breakfast, ran out after me.

"I know we must have been a sight," I told my son, and I chuckled. "Me sitting in this tree, with my powder-blue party dress on, and Aunt Loretta standing at the bottom begging for me to come on down."

But again I refused. This went on for days; the only time I would come down was at night, when I would eat and then fall into an exhausted sleep. And each morning, more of me was gone.

On the fifth day, some womenfolk came by the house in the afternoon; they had heard about what was happening to me. I could hear them talking on the porch. Every now and then one of them would look over at the tree, where I sat hidden in the leaves, and shake her head.

"She needs a whupping," Mrs. Fuller said. She was Aunt Loretta's best friend. She knew how to handle children, since she had four girls around my same age, and Aunt Loretta had never had a one.

When they had each given my aunt an opinion on what she should do with me, they made their way down the driveway, still chattering.

"Always knew that child was different," one said.

"Just like her momma."

"Mm-hmm."

Their words drifted up and covered me like a blanket. That evening, when Aunt Loretta came to keep me company, I whispered down so that she had to get up on the tips of her toes to hear me. "She ain't coming back, is she?"

Aunt Loretta just looked up into the tree, her dark, sad eyes peering into mine.

"I want to tell you a story, Pontella, about this tree you sittin' in." She sighed and settled down among the tangle of roots overgrown with velvety green moss, into the seatlike crook that had formed at the base of the tree.

"There was this girl named Wheat, a slave girl who came to live here on this very land. It used to belong to a family called the Brantleys. But then their children grew older and moved on. Left the place to their driver, your granddaddy.

"At first no one knew her name or how old she was, though they could tell she was a child-woman; they knew none of the things most folks know about a person. But she entered this place in the back of a wagon, and before it was all said and done they would know more than they could ever forget.

"It all started when the old Master died. His son, the young Master, went and found himself a wife, who wanted a girl for herself. They already had the old woman Lettie, who worked in the house, and Lettie's son Jonathan, who worked the fields. Wasn't enough for the Missus.

"You know how folks is: if somebody else have two slaves, they gotta have three. Like when Mr. Bubby bought that car a few years back, and then all the men around here had to go buy themselves one. I tell ya, folks the same everywhere.

"So the Missus had to have a girl, a personal slave girl. As a weddin' gift, young Master went down to South Carolina one day and came back with this girl in the back of the wagon. Even with her hands bound with rope, tied to the side of the cart, there was somethin' about her that said she wasn't nobody's slave. Her face was raised up to the sun so that she appeared as if she had been dipped in gold. Her hair was soft like a baby's but thick as rope, and it streamed behind her and up into the air as if it were oil-blackened flames. And tall: when the Master unloosed her hands and she unfolded herself from that wagon, she shot up like a stalk of wheat, see? She knew that she had another name, though, and when the wind stirred up the leaves or the rain pelted its melody into the dust, they murmured that name for her.

"Wheat became the Missus's girl. Worked in the house and in the evenins she would sit with Lettie, never sayin' a word, just sittin' while the old woman cleaned the kitchen and caught up with that day's darnin' and other sewin'. Then the two would retire, Lettie to her cabin and Wheat upstairs to sleep at the foot of the Missus's bed on a makeshift pallet of blankets. They all thought the girl had settled into the place. But one mornin' they awoke to find that she had disappeared, run off.

"Master got the hounds on her, and they found her holed up in a hollow of trees on the way to Pennsylvania. They brought her back, once again tied to the back of the wagon, but this time when the Master unloosed her hands, it was only to bring her to this tree. He wrapped her arms around it so she hugged the base, and stripped her so her back was bare. Whupped that gal, the lash a tongue that licked the golden skin from her body until her blood ran down and mingled with the wet grass.

"Lettie took care of her, fixed her up, the raw wounds

turnin' into a tangle of roots that would forever remind Wheat of the day she became one with the trees.

"After that beatin', the Master figured that girl wasn't goin' nowhere. But one mornin' about six months later, they woke up to find the foot of Missus's bed empty again. Again the Master went out after her, and they found her, this time headin' back down south.

"They ripped out one of her front teeth so she'd be easier to find next time. When they brought her back, the blood had already crusted into the corners of her mouth and chin. The trappers, who had helped the Master find Wheat, had this contraption called the grave, which they gave to the Master so he could break the girl. It was the length of a coffin, with small holes in the top. At the end where the head went was a slot the width of a grown man's fist. That was so they could pass in food and water. But as soon as the meal was done, the little door in the slot was sealed shut again. Nothing but darkness. The only time Wheat would get to see the sunlight was when they fed her. Didn't even let her out to relieve herself.

"They put Wheat inside that thing facedown and kept her there for ten days. Kept her in that tight space of darkness until she didn't know the days from the years, kept her until she didn't know herself from the blackness. Until she dissolved and became air. At night Lettie would sometimes sneak out of her cabin to go talk to the girl, but the hauntin' moans that came from that box frightened her so much she couldn't move. When they did let Wheat out, she wasn't quite the same. Even still, we knew it was only a matter of time before she ran again. It was the way she moved: held her body like one of them horses that couldn't be broken, the way her muscles rippled beneath her skin at just the slightest word or touch.

"The Master was near about desperate. Wheat would look up at times durin' the day and find his eyes on her, tryin' to capture her. She had begun talkin' to the sunlight and the grass, the wind. They told her things. She stopped sittin' with Lettie in the evenins and never would go around Jonathan.

"Lettie and Jonathan thought the girl was crazy. But Wheat knew what they were sayin'; the wind told her everything. What they didn't know was how her skin hurt when they got too close. So she took to conversin' with the grass and listened to the trees instead. They told her about the white people and this thing called slavery, how it had come from inside of her, inside all of them. It had been created out of the bleakest part of their souls. And she had the power to uncreate it.

"Not long after, the Master gave Wheat a cabin of her own. She knew that sooner or later he would move through the night and make his way to her. That's why she wasn't at all surprised to see the door open to a silent figure that slipped into her night-shrouded room. She waited until he came to stand at the foot of her bed. Her eyes glittered like a barn owl's, watchin'. Then she began to laugh what sounded like the hissin' of a thousand snakes.

"She reared up from the bed and thrust her face into the Master's. 'I take you back,' she spat at him. 'I take back your soul.' Her hands reached out like talons as he stumbled away from the bed, from the room and its curse. The color had drained from his face, and Jonathan, who was sittin' outside his own cabin, thought at first the old Master had risen from the dead.

"He left Wheat pretty much alone after that, sent her out to work the fields with Jonathan, but she didn't mind. She loved bein' in the sunlight, where she could talk to the things outdoors and listen for when it was time for her to leave again.

"It was Jonathan that did it. He worked side by side with the strange girl, and after a while he, too, started to listen. During the day he would move so that he could be closer to Wheat while they worked, and at night he would sit outside her cabin door and speak in tones that sounded like the rustlin' of wind through new spring leaves, until Wheat's ears grew eager for his words.

"Then one night a squall blew in. It was one of those fierce summer storms that rage as if to consume everything in their path, only to rush back out again in a matter of moments. When it was over, Wheat waited on the edge of her bed, her heart racin'. She wanted Jonathan to come with his words that quieted her, and it was then she figured out what the storm had been sayin', what the Master was doin'. How he was usin' Jonathan this time. A yearnin' she had never felt before told her how they wanted to get her with child. She could almost feel the sharp hooks of a child's cry pierce her breasts, keep her from goin' away. When Jonathan finally did come, Wheat stuffed herself into the corner of the room, her hands over her ears. He whispered to her. His words scurried under the cracks in the door and into the room. Crawled over to where she crouched huddled in the blackness, tremblin'.

"She waited until he was gone before she left her cabin. When she came out, it was to this tree. The moonlight streamed through the branches with a light so pure she could feel it openin' up the hidden places inside of her. She could hear the tree, its blood, her blood coursin' like a river, and she knew it was time for her to go.

"Sometime within that moment when the darkness separates itself from the dawn, a stillness fell over this place, over the earth, the entire universe. It was as if God himself mourned. That's what woke up the Master and the Missus, Jonathan and Lettie. They saw it at the same time. What used to be a girl called Wheat. How she had become one with the tree, her body a broken, swingin' branch that almost touched the ground."

Aunt Loretta got up, stretched herself, and went into the house, leaving me alone in Wheat's tree—my tree. The sun was still out, though the sky contained just a hint of orange and purple that signified the coming twilight. Hesitantly, I climbed down. I could finally see my bony knees that turned inward and almost touched each other, my dusty feet as I followed Aunt Loretta into our home.

"It never left me, the feeling that I would wake up one day and no one would be able to see me. Not until the day I had you." I pointed toward the bedroom window. "You were born right in that room up there."

I lifted my son, who had fallen asleep, out of the wagon and positioned him so he lay across my shoulder. "The very moment you left the place you had been and entered the room, a quiet fell, broken only by your mewling cry," I continued in a whisper.

"I understood then what Wheat knew: you were a hook. But I also found out what she and my mother would never come to know: sometimes a hook is the one thing, the only thing, that can keep you from becoming invisible."

ACORN PIPES

Hiron Jackson Fuller died on the second Friday in March, but it was already as warm as a day in June—unseasonably warm. The time of year when Ma'D would normally have her girls, Hira, Cinny, Cease, and Tavi, getting the house ready for the coming of a new spring. Cinny and Hira, the two oldest, would help Ma'D wash, dry, and iron the white sheer curtains to replace the heavy drapes that blocked out the winter sun along with cold drafts of air. That was the part Hira loved best. Feeling the light folds of material spill out over the skin of her honey-colored arms. For hours she would pretend she was a bride, the curtains her train. Or a princess in royal garb. Hira lived on such illusions.

But this year they hadn't been doing any of that; they had been making the house ready for their daddy, who lay in the parlor for his three days of viewing.

Uncle Clarence, Hiron's friend since the war, had come up from the city once he got word. Helped Ma'D prepare the body with herbs and sweet oils like the old way. They dressed him in his one good suit. Placed him in the box Uncle Clarence had built with his own hands, tears rolling into the deep lines of his grief-ravaged face.

The night before the funeral, Hira snuck downstairs to see him. It didn't really look much like her daddy. More like something had eased into his skin while he was sleeping. It was the same broad nose, all right, but the lips and cheeks were a little too sunk-in to belong. New pennies had been taped over his eyes—for what, Hira couldn't quite remember.

Hira had placed a blanket around him the way Cinny used to do whenever he was too sickly to make it up to bed and fell asleep on the kitchen floor instead. Someone had removed it sometime since then. Tossed it on the sofa, where it lay crumpled and abandoned.

Hira sat in the kitchen with the rest of her sisters as the men who had come to carry the coffin made their way to the front room. They was Hiron's "swingin' buddies," as he used to say. The ones he played poker with or sat with in front of the town's barber shop, swapping lies. Shameless, from what Ma'D and most other folks said. To Hira they looked as foreign as her daddy, dressed up in too-tight or too-long suits and scuffed-toed work boots.

The four girls waited in the kitchen, hands folded in their laps, while the pallbearers struggled to get the coffin out through the dining room. The box was long, so as to fit their daddy's frame, and the men struggled within the confines of the tight farmhouse. Ma'D could be heard directing the six men which way to twist themselves so as not to bump into any of her family portraits or the china closet filled with all types of cheap miniature knickknacks. Judging by the bumps against the wall that separated the dining room from the kitchen, they was trying to stay as far away from that side of the room as possible.

That'd be all Ma'D needed, for Hiron Fuller to ruin the last of what little bit she had. She would have blamed him for trying to take it all with him, like she used to do whenever they argued about the money he spent on his nights out.

Once they finally got past the threshold of the kitchen, it was no time before they was all heading out the door, the men carrying the weight on their shoulders, three on each side, the box swaying between them. Ma'D followed not more than two steps behind, flanked on either side by two girls, her face hidden by the veil of her hat. She wore the only black dress she owned, a heavy wool frock that buttoned up to the very top of her neck, making her appear smaller than she actually was.

With heads down, they moved toward the circular driveway off to the left side of the farmhouse. They had to take the road instead of cutting across the Pinder place like they usually did when heading to church. The small crest of land that formed a slight hill would have made it almost impossible for the men to carry their burden through the waist-high fields. By the time the family reached the lilac bushes that marked the end of the driveway, a tight cluster of town folks had already gathered. As Ma'D and her girls turned onto the graveled road, the crowd of mourners filed in behind.

Hira turned around to catch sight of the ladies who had come to the house during the week to bring food and whisper with Ma'D in the front room. She was used to seeing them working their own gardens and fields, hearing them holler at her as she made her way past their houses off to school or play. The women here today were impostors, with somber faces and thin-lipped grimaces where smiles and laughter usually resided. Hira couldn't pull herself away from the sight of these women until Ma'D near about shook her arm loose. Could almost hear her mother saying how "it's just not polite to stare at folks," forcing Hira to turn back toward the coffin's rising and falling, like breathing. Someone started singing in a voice so clear it competed with the March birds:

> *Oh, the old ark's movin', movin', movin',*
> *the old ark's movin',*
> *and I's goin' on home.*

Then the men joined in, their baritones rushing in to settle beneath the high, clear trill of the lead singer.

> *See that brotha there comin' so slow?*
> *He wants to gets to Heaven 'fo' the*
> *Heaven doors close.*
> *'Tain't but one thin' on my mind:*
> *brotha's gone to Heaven and left me behind.*

The crowd of people dispersed as the procession entered the churchyard. The song faded into the air as Ma'D, Uncle Clarence, and the four girls made their way inside to take their places in the row reserved for the family. Hiron's coffin was set down at the altar, nested between vibrant flowers shaped into a bleeding heart and a variety of crosses, their thick fragrances hanging in the church's hot air. The town folks filed by to view the body, some commenting on how lifelike "the May-a" looked laying there.

After a while, Reverend Snowden stood up in the pulpit with his best robe on, a stirring figure. So light he looked like a white man, except he had the nappiest head of hair anyone had ever seen. It was the color of red sand. Looked like rusted steel wool sitting up there on his head. Clusters of freckles made up his face, like God had taken a shaker of cinnamon and sprinkled some on his nose and cheeks. He was a natural-born preacher man, folks said. Had the kind of voice that would take hold of you and shake you up. How it would rise and fall, cresting like waves, and by the end of the service his words would be stuck in your head like a tune that couldn't get loose.

It wasn't until Reverend Snowden's thunder-filled voice boomed out over the heads of the people that a hush fell throughout the congregation. He asked that all bow their heads in prayer as they started the home-going service for Hiron Fuller.

"We thank the Lawd for this day, such a beautiful day to usher one of our own home. Hiron Fuller was a good man. A hardworkin' man. Loved his family. His wife, four beautiful daughters, and a host of friends. He loved this town. But most of all, brotha Fuller loved the Lawd. And it was Him that called His child to come and sit by His side. In Jesus' name we say Amen."

"Amen," the crowd echoed while Reverend Snowden took his seat. Miss Ruth got up to sing one of Ma'D's favorite songs, something about a sparrow, but Hira, who had sat up in her seat when the preacher started talking, couldn't stop thinking about what he had just said. She thought, Daddy *was* a good man. He loved *all* of us. The preacher said so, and everyone knows a preacher man speaks for God. And God don't lie. Coming from Reverend Snowden, it must be Truth.

Hira saw Uncle Clarence get up from the pew and make his way to the podium to read the obituary. He had been her daddy's closest friend; surely he would be able to tell her about the man who now lay in that box. But instead he talked about how Hiron Fuller had married Dorothy Coombs before going off to serve his country in the army. Didn't mention how Hiron was regulated to a driver, who learned how to play poker and drink liquor and ended up taking most of his friends' money come check day. Talked about how close Hiron was to his daughters, especially Cinny. How folks called him the May-a. Went through Hiron Fuller's whole life in a matter of minutes.

When Uncle Clarence was finished, he went back to his seat as the church choir broke out into another song. Their voices, mixed with the growing heat inside the church and the swish of wooden fans, lulled Hira into near sleep. Deacon Weems read one of the psalms, and there was more singing. But when the preacher man came back to the pulpit, Hira scooted to the edge of the pew. She had been waiting for something all day, though she didn't know quite what it was.

Reverend Snowden had them turn to Ecclesiastes 7:1–14. Everyone retrieved a Bible from the shelf in front of them, except Hira. She didn't dare move. Never took her eyes from the man in that pulpit. She waited, afraid to breathe lest she miss what the man of God had to say about her daddy. Secrets she needed to hear:

> *A good name is better than*
> *a good ointment,*
> *And the day of one's*
> *death is better than*
> *the day of one's birth . . .*

On and on Reverend Snowden read, interjecting into his recital grunts and groans and emphatic "amens" that were echoed by the congregation. And still Hira didn't hear what she had been waiting for. When it was over, she sagged against the pew. She felt full up and empty all at the same time. Wanted to crawl underneath the bench in front of her and curl up into a tight ball and sleep.

"Don't wait to get right with the Lawd," the reverend urged. "Look at brotha Fuller. Dint know when he went to do a day of decent, hard work that he would never again see the light of day. Dint know that the Lawd was gonna call him home! And neither do you know the day nor the hour when it's *yo'* time to go on home."

It was enough to make grown men weep. The preacher

used Hiron Fuller's home-going service to deliver one of his best sermons. By the time he was done, four town folks was filled with the Spirit and ran up to the altar to confess their sinful ways, give their lives to Christ. All on account of Hiron Fuller got drunk, went out to cut some trees, and accidentally cut his leg near about off. Bled to death.

After the preaching part of the funeral, Ma'D had her best friend, Miss Loretta, take Hira and her sisters back to the house. She didn't want them to see their daddy get buried. Didn't want them to remember him that way. The walk home took no time at all compared to when they started out that morning. None of the girls said a word, each surrendered to her own thoughts, Hira thinking over her daddy's service. Only Miss Loretta rambled on, trying to make the girls feel better about having to put their daddy in the ground.

"Your daddy loved you girls so much. Was a real good man," she said to no one in particular.

"Our daddy was a drinkin' man, Miss Loretta. A gamblin' man, too," Cinny said.

"Why, Miss Cinny. You not supposed to talk thataway about the dead; they can hear you, you know. And I know your mother raised you better than that."

"Well, the way everybody talkin', our daddy's a king of Egypt or sumptin. But our momma was the one who called him a drunk every time he come home smellin' like whiskey," Cinny replied.

"Hush up, child. Here, we home. Just go on in the house and change out of your good clothes. Go on, all of you girls."

Hira had seen how Miss Loretta tried to keep from laughing out loud. Just like their daddy used to do whenever Cinny said something that tickled him. Hira had to swallow to keep from slapping Cinny's face as she ran to catch up with the rest of her sisters.

When the girls was done changing, they all came to sit out on the screened porch. The wood floor had been painted the same green as the farmhouse, the color of new honeydew melon. There was deep scratches in some places where the paint had been scraped off, showing the color beneath, a steel gray. From where the girls sat, Hira and Tavi on the white metal porch swing, Cinny and Cease in two folding chairs on the other side of the porch, they could smell the scent of cherry blossoms that floated through with each casual breeze. Even still, there was a tension in the air, the crackling that comes before a spring storm.

" 'Member the stories Daddy told us about the little men who lived in the woods and smoked rabbit tobaccer in their little acorn pipes? How he tried to make those same pipes when he was a boy?" Hira asked her sisters.

"Yeah. We remember," Cinny answered, not looking up from where she sat picking at the fresh scabs on her elbows and knees. "But they was just fairy tales."

"Well, you can say what you want, but he taught me how to make them acorn pipes."

"When?" Cinny looked over in Hira's direction, a hint of scorn in the pout of her lips.

"When he took me fishin' and huntin'."

"Daddy ain't take you fishin', Hira. You always makin' stuff up," Tavi said.

"I ain't," Hira snapped.

"Well, I don't remember Daddy ever takin' nobody no-wheres but Cinny. And Ma'D, when they wasn't fussin'."

Hira could feel her ears grow hot. She stared at her sisters, eyes slitted as if staring into the sun. "Well, he did. And he taught me how to make acorn pipes, just like I said."

Cinny said they should go make some, have a good smoke themselves. Hira lowered her eyes down to her hands.

"Well?" Cinny dared.

Hira jumped up from the swing. "All right, then. I'll teach y'all myself."

She left the porch, with the other girls following right be-hind, to hunt around the oak tree in the yard. They all spread out in the grass, searching, like young birds looking for rain worms.

"Here, this is a good one. Find one like this." Hira held a plump acorn between her two fingers. "Not too small."

They kept on looking until each girl had found a good-sized acorn of her own. When they was done, they handed the nuts to Hira so she could stuff them into the pockets of her coveralls. All except Cinny. Always Cinny.

"Now we've gotta go to the creek and get some reeds."

"We can't go to the creek 'thout askin' Ma'D first, Hira," Cease reminded her sister.

"Looka here, Ma'D is tied up with shakin' everybody's hands and hearin' them talk about how sorry they is about Daddy. She ain't thinkin' about us."

Cinny crossed both arms across her chest, hands resting underneath her armpits. "I ain't goin' nowheres, and neither is Tavi and Cease. You don't know the first thing about makin' no acorn pipes."

Hira could feel anger rush up from her belly, closing off her throat.

"That's right," Cinny continued. "I'm tired of this foolishness. You know daggone well Daddy ain't never taught you how to make no acorn pipes. His hands shook so he could barely write his own name. Now, I'm hungry and hot and—"

Before Cinny could finish, Hira, who had balled her hands into fists, rushed across the grass and slammed into the soft flesh of Cinny's belly, knocking the air out of her with a loud whoosh. Cinny fell backward onto the ground and lay there for a few moments, dazed. Tavi and Cease, as if on cue, put both hands across their mouths, the look on Cinny's face reflecting the shock they all felt. Nobody had ever hit Cinny like that—nobody except Ma'D, and she didn't count.

Then Cinny jumped up and pointed her finger at Hira as she screamed in her face, "Don't ya ever, ever put your hands on me thataway." What looked like tears welled up in Cinny's eyes, though it was a long time since anyone had seen her cry.

Hira could only stand there, her face set in determination, waiting for the blow she knew would come. Instead, Cinny turned to run back to the farmhouse, stopping just to spin back around and chuck her acorn hard as she could, at her sister, hitting Hira in the corner of her left eye. "You ain't nothin' but a damned liar. Wouldn't know the truth if it sat down beside ya!"

Hira didn't move. Just stood there like she was frozen until Cinny disappeared inside the house. Then she bent down and picked up what she thought was Cinny's acorn. Looked at Tavi and Cease as if daring them to move.

"Come on," Hira demanded, heading in the direction of the creek. She moved on quickened, almost desperate feet. Tavi and Cease followed behind like they was being led someplace they had never been to before, trying their best to keep up.

After a near-frantic search at the creek, Hira and her sisters made their way back to the farmhouse, reeds in hand.

"Hira, let's go to the hidey-out?" Tavi suggested, more a pleading than anything else. She had never seen her sister act like this.

"That's a good idea."

By the time they reached the house, Hira saw that the grown folks had come back from the graveyard. Their hidey-out was the space underneath the back porch. She got down on her hands and knees and crawled behind the porch's cement stairs. Tavi and Cease copied her.

It was dark and cool inside, a place hidden from both the heat of the day and the watchful eye of the grown folks. Hira sat down with her legs crossed on the hard-packed earth. The only light was from the sun that sprinkled in through the lattice boards skirting the sides of the porch. Tavi and Cease sat near enough to Hira to see what their oldest sister was doing. Hira pulled an acorn from her pocket and laid it in her lap while she got out her miniature penknife. The penknife used to belong to Cinny. Their daddy had won it at the York Fair the summer before, playing the ring-toss game. Hira had traded her sister a baby frog for the knife, but about a week after the trade, the frog had escaped, making Hira feel like she had gotten the better end of the bargain. Hira wished Cinny could be there to see her make that pipe, just like she'd told her she could.

She cut the top off of the acorn, its cap already gone. From where she sat, Hira could hear some of the grown folks spilling onto the back porch. Could hear them talking about the funeral service. These was the same voices that had sang Hiron Fuller's marching song on the way to the church that morning. Someone commented on how nice the funeral had been.

"Reverend Snowden sho did preach up a storm."

"Mm-hmm. Sure did."

She thought about the other quick snatches of words she had heard since Friday. So many pieces to fit together. She wondered just what her daddy would have thought about all this.

"So what really happened to the May-a?"

Hira could have told all of them what had happened. But they wouldn't have believed her anyway. She knew that he had got up early that last morning and left with his work mule, Walter P., to do a job over on the other side of Moss Woods for Mr. Richards. Had to clear some trees off the property so Mr. Richards could build a place for his only daughter and her new husband. Hiron had taken the job the week before, after Ma'D laid into him because of another one of his sicknesses.

"He was doing a job for Mr. Richards."

Hira could see her daddy, tall and gangly but strong,

swinging that ax of his. Each movement capturing the glint of the sun. Powerful strokes, a sheen of sweat making him glow in the day's light. She could hear him whistling like he always did whenever he was doing honest work.

"I hear tell a tree fell on 'im."

She could see the blow that slipped. How it glanced out of the V cut into the tree's trunk to embed itself in her daddy's leg. Could see him laying on the ground, not knowing what to do. And no one to help him,

"Naw, chile. He was drunk. As usual!"

except for Walter P., who would have been standing somewhere nearby, unmindful of what was going on,

"Somebody said they found him laid up against a tree in a pool of blood."

chewing on some grass, probably, large eyes blinking like he hadn't a care. When Walter P. didn't come, her daddy would have crawled, his hands gouging the warm,

"Smellin' like a still. Jug right beside him."

moist earth just to get back to his girls, and especially her, the one he had forgotten to tell everything he wanted her to know. The one who carried his name,

"It's shameless. He was shameless."

Hira. whose name she was sure was the last word to fall from his lips, an agonized whisper—

"Poor Dorothy. Those poor chirrun."

Hira's hands shook as she tried to hold on to the acorn. She began to dig the meat of the nut from where it nestled inside the shell.

"That man was a damned fool, is what."

After cleaning all the meat out of the acorn shell, she took the tip of her knife and began to make a small hole where the reed would go.

"Loved his whiskey, that's fo' sho."

Laughter rippled throughout the group, filtered through the slits in the wood floor, and covered the girls like grains of dirt.

Gently, Hira twisted the tip of the knife to widen the hole she was trying to make. She felt the shell begin to splinter in her hand until all that was left was a handful of jagged pieces and a small pile of soft, fine dust. Hira opened her fingers to let the debris fall onto the unyielding ground. She put her head on her knees and wrapped her arms around them, the sobs shaking her body.

"Lawd, they better off without 'im."

ALL THAT'S LEFT

Junie threw the baseball to Sonny Fisher with all the force she could muster. "I could kill that girl!"

"What she do now?" Scoogie asked from where he sat on the porch steps.

Junie turned to face the older boy. "Tried to act like she wanted to be my friend." She threw the baseball back to Sonny. "Can you believe that? How sneaky can a person be?"

Sonny tossed the ball to the other boys, Georgie and Timothy Henson, identical twins except for the banana-shaped birthmark on the side of Timothy's face, and Dennis Fisher, Sonny's little brother. The six were an odd mixture of playmates, friends mainly because they happened to have been born around the same time and lived in the same small town, Grandville, Maryland. Junie, the only girl, and Scoogie, the oldest by sixteen months, were the ones who vied for the role of leader of the little gang, the position having been traded back and forth between the two throughout the years until they found themselves at a point of impasse.

The three youngest boys, Dennis and the twins, scooped up their gloves and a bat from the grass and ran off to the center of the yard to practice hitting. They had all heard Junie's complaints about Pontella before. Everyone knew about the feud between the two girls. How it had reached the level of civil war, at least in the minds of thirteen-year-old girls, who developed battle strategies the same way they prepared for backyard games.

Junie and Sonny went over to Scoogie. The older boy had once been Junie's best friend, but two weeks ago she had walked up on the group of boys as they waited for her in the baseball field and caught Scoogie talking about her. She didn't know what he had been saying, but an awkwardness, one that had never before existed among the six of them, had fallen over the group, so that the others could hardly look her in the eye.

"You girls are so stupid," Scoogie said, smirking at Sonny as he came to lean against the porch railing. Junie knew that Scoogie's view of girls came from his father, a drunk who beat his wife and daughters whenever the hooch got to him. But she didn't say any of this; instead she sat down on the edge of the step and thought about Pontella.

Pontella was the one couldn't be trusted. The girl had embarrassed Junie in front of the fellas that time, the first time Junie sprang the tree maneuver on her. Pontella, tattletale that she was, ran home to her high-siddity aunt Loretta. Before Junie could get through laughing at the sight of the girl's face when the acorns struck her, and climb down from the tree, Miss Loretta was standing underneath. That woman had started screaming at Junie, going on about her being no-account nigger trash, even though everyone knew it was *Pontella's* mother, Ebbie Pinder, who had run off all those years ago and come back to Grandville with a baby in tow and no husband, only to sneak off again not even three years later.

And Pontella standing there like the cat that lapped the cream while her aunt went up one side of Junie and down the other. When Junie decided to get down from the tree and take the whuppin' she knew was coming, that should have been the end of it. Except Pontella went up to the schoolyard and started running off at the mouth.

When they got to the schoolyard, Pontella went to join the older girls, and Junie to stand with the fellas clustered at the foot of the hill that rose behind the schoolhouse. Pontella could be overheard telling her audience about what had just happened. Junie didn't give a lick about the Miss Prisses; it was when she looked around at the boys and saw them trying to hold back their laughter that she wanted to slap Pontella's mouth shut. But Pontella just kept on, pretending like she wasn't talking to Junie, and Junie pretending like she wasn't hearing a word. And then Junie heard Pontella calling her names like "vermin" and "trash." She said that Junie's new name was June Bug because she was nothing more than a insect, just like her aunt Loretta had said.

Now Pontella was acting like she wanted to be Junie's friend. If there was one thing Junie could count on, it was how much she hated that girl. The very sight of those pin curls and cute bobby socks made her so mad she could spit. But if she had wanted to, Junie could have remembered a time when the two had been friends, chasing fireflies and rabbits in each other's outdoors.

"Pontella's the one that's stupid." Junie crossed her arms over her chest. "If she think I'ma fall for her tricks."

"You should get back at her," Scoogie said.

"Don't worry, I will."

"How?" the boy challenged.

"I'll think of somethin'."

Junie watched as Dennis tried to hit Georgie's so-called fastball. Each time the ball whizzed by, Dennis would swing the bat, so that in no time at all he had struck out and was flinging the bat to the ground in frustration.

"I know a way you could get her," Scoogie said.

"How, Scoogie?" Sonny moved closer to the older boy.

"Just have her come up to old man Alvin's barn."

"Why?" Junie asked.

"Look, you get her up there and we be ready for her."

"To do what, Scoogie?" Sonny asked.

"Scare her, is all," Scoogie said, staring at Junie with a smile on his face. She was the first to turn away. She looked over at Timothy, Georgie, and Dennis, who were oblivious to everything except their game. Junie thought about this past Saturday, when the six of them had played football along with a couple of other boys from the neighborhood. How Scoogie had tackled her, stayed on top of her until she thought she would scream. His deceptively thin body was heavy; it'd made it hard for her to breathe. Made her feel like she was drowning.

"You won't hurt her, Scoogie?" Junie kept her eyes on the younger boys a few moments longer before turning back to gaze at him. "That's all I need. Mama's already mad at me on account of this Pontella thing."

"I won't hurt her. Just teach her a lesson."

"How'm I gonna get her up there? Pontella ain't gon' believe nothin' I have to say."

"You'll come up with somethin' good. I know you, Junie Mason."

Junie looked at the boy at her side, then at Sonny, then at the others. These were the same boys she had played with all her life, the same boys she used to swim naked with in the creek. She looked back at Scoogie. Started shaking her head.

"We ain't never knowed you to back outta nothin'," Scoogie quickly interrupted before Junie could get a chance to open her mouth.

"All right, then." Junie got up from the step and dusted off the seat of her coveralls. "Get the rest of the fellas, and I'll meet y'all up there."

"With Pontella," Scoogie stressed before he and Sonny ran over to where the other boys played.

Junie watched them whispering together for a few minutes before she took off down the graveled driveway. She looked back in time to see the five boys heading up the slight hill that separated Mr. Alvin's land from the Fishers'.

Junie already knew how she could get Pontella to come

with her to Mr. Alvin's. Everybody knew about the one thing that could get to Pontella, and that was her mother. That and hair.

Just the day before, Junie and Pontella had met up on that same road as they made their way home from school. At first they had walked in a constricted silence, until Pontella made mention of how nice Junie's hair was, how Junie had "probably the prettiest hair in the whole town."

Tryin' to get on my good side, Junie thought, cutting her eyes at the other girl.

"I could do something with it if you wanted," Pontella went on.

"Like what?" Junie asked.

Pontella chatted about the fashion magazines her aunt Loretta had bought for her, saying how she had seen some hairstyles that would be perfect for Junie's thick, wavy hair. She wondered why Junie still wore her hair in pigtails, when every other girl their age had gone to curls. The two of them went on and on until they got to the Mason place.

Junie looked over now at Moss Woods as she made her way down the road. The trees had already begun to turn; their orange and rust-colored leaves flickered against the backdrop of the sky.

She reached up and grabbed one of her pigtails. Her sun-warmed hair moved fluidly between her fingers as she undid the plait. In a matter of seconds, her hair flowed unheeded down to the small of her back. Anyone who had walked by at that moment would have been surprised to discover that this was the same Junie Mason who played football and baseball like one of the boys. With her hair like this, she conjured a womanly air far more pronounced than the studied maturity of Pontella and the other neighborhood girls.

It wasn't too far to the Pinders'. In a place like Grandville, where time was measured by how long it took the sun to sink to the bottom of the sky, and distance by the steps it took to get to someone's yard, the Pinders, who lived about ten minutes from the Fishers, were considered their next-door neighbors. In no time at all Junie could see the two stone pillars that marked the entry to the Pinders' property. She made her way past the front of the house as if she visited Pontella *every* Saturday in the late afternoon. No one except the occasional out-of-towner used a person's front door.

Junie strode onto the screened porch and knocked on the back door. It wasn't long before Miss Loretta came to the doorway in a flowered print dress of pinks and reds that sagged at her chest and hugged her wide hips. She wore her hair in pin curls, and Junie could see how Pontella had come to wear her own.

"Afternoon, Miss Lo-retta." Junie stood on the porch, both hands twisting the sides of her coveralls. "I came to see Pontella."

Pontella's aunt stuck her head out the door and peered into Junie's face. "June Mason? Well, I'll be." Satisfied that this was indeed the Mason girl, she settled back into her doorway as if on duty. "What you want with my niece? Trouble?"

"Naw, ma'am, Miss Lo-retta. The other day Pontella offered to do me a favor. And I'm meanin' to take her up on it."

"You can come in, but you wait right here. I'ma go find Pontella and see what she say about this."

Junie pulled her shoulders together and squeezed between the doorjamb and Miss Loretta to stand in the Pinders' kitchen. Miss Loretta went out of the room in search of her niece. Junie pushed her sweating hands underneath the bib of her coveralls and wiped them on her T-shirt.

The spacious kitchen housed a table large enough to seat a family of six, though only Pontella and her aunt lived here. The wall opposite Junie sported two windows that extended almost from floor to ceiling, and with the curtains pulled back, the robin's-egg-blue walls shone bright in the remaining sunlight.

It wasn't too long before Pontella entered the room, wearing the same outfit Junie had seen her in the day before. The black skirt with not one but three red poodles and the white bobby socks both made her appear younger than she was.

"Junie? What you doing here? I didn't believe my auntie when she said it was you wanting to see me."

"Um, Pontella, I told your aunt I needed a favor. Remember yesterday when you said you could do somethin' with my hair?"

"Yes, I remember."

"Well, if your aunt would have asked me, I was going to tell her that I had come for that. But . . ." Junie ran her fingers over her hair.

Pontella's gaze followed those fingers, as if she was noticing for the first time the absence of pigtails. Her own hand flew upward as if to touch Junie's hair. "Why, Junie Mason, it's even prettier than I thought!" Pontella exclaimed. "You said there was a 'but,' though."

"That's right. I didn't really come for that. That was just

to throw your aunt off. I came to get you so you could see something."

"What?"

Junie dropped her voice to a whisper as she leaned toward the other girl. "Dead body behind Mr. Alvin's barn."

"What!" Pontella's eyes widened in horror, and she leaned even closer to Junie.

"Ssh. You don't want your aunt to hear."

Pontella looked at Junie with squinted eyes. She cocked her head to the side and pursed her lips. "Why should I believe you, Junie Mason?"

"I mean, ya know, if you scared." Junie turned as if to leave.

"I ain't scared. It just don't sound right. Why don't the grown folks know? Aunt Loretta ain't said nothing about it. And why you come get *me*?"

"That's because some of the boys found it. Just this morning. Figured the person was passing by Mr. Alvin's late last night. Coming this way, probably. And . . . it's a woman. Boys say a strange woman, ain't none of them ever seen her before. For some reason I thought of you, that's all."

Pontella's face had brightened. Her eyes shone with an eagerness she couldn't quite disguise. "Well, OK, but let me tell Auntie where I'm going." And she left the room.

For a brief moment Junie felt like running. She even reached for the handle on the screen door, but before she could make up her mind to go, the girl was back in the kitchen. She grabbed Junie by the arm and steered her out of the house.

Once they were outside, Pontella released her, and the two made their way from the Pinders' yard. Neither spoke at first.

"A dead body?" Pontella said after a minute or two.

"That's what the fellas said."

"I ain't never seen a dead body before. Except at funerals. But that don't count, do it?"

"Naw, it don't."

"And it's a woman?"

"That's what the fellas say. A strange woman," Junie said again.

"Umm." Pontella nodded her head.

The two girls walked along in silence for a while.

Pontella looked at Junie. "I really like doing hair, ya know."

Junie kept her eyes on the road, her hair forming a curtain around the contours of her face. She watched as the dust rose and settled over the toes of her work boots.

"That's what I want to do when I grow up, hair. But Auntie wants me to be a teacher or a nurse. I did hers, though. You like it?"

Junie realized the other girl had asked her a question. "Huh?"

"Did you like it?"

"Like what?"

"My auntie's hair. I did it."

"Oh, yeah. I thought maybe *she* did *yours*. I like it."

Pontella nodded her head and smiled. Settled back into the silence. The sun had continued its movement across the sky, bringing with it the first signs of dusk. The chatter of leaves disquieted by the day's winds softened into a hum.

"My momma used to brush my hair when I was a little girl. Auntie says I was too young to remember that, but I do." There was a wistfulness in Pontella's voice.

Junie looked over at her as if seeing her for the first time. She wanted to tell the girl about her own father. Wanted to tell her how she had got her womanlies already. How her daddy wouldn't let her sit on his lap anymore. Wouldn't hold her like he used to.

"I know," Junie began. But then the hill that led to Mr. Alvin's appeared over Pontella's right shoulder. "We're here." Junie pointed in that direction.

Pontella turned her head. "Oh, Lord," she said, placing her hands across her pounding heart.

"We gotta run," Junie said. "We can slow down once we get past Mr. Alvin, who I'm sure is sitting at that window waiting to catch somebody cutting through his yard." She grabbed Pontella by the arm. "Come on."

The two took off in a peal of nervous giggles, running past the odd-shaped hedges, the washed-out gray of old man Alvin's house, and the dark face that appeared between parted curtains at one of the windows. It wasn't until they reached the back of the property, the barn now in sight, that Junie slowed to let Pontella to take the lead.

The neglected barn stood forlorn at the edge of a field. Moss shrouded the building, painting it a dreary green. Loose boards gaped like missing teeth, a sinister grin spreading throughout the barn's construction. Junie lagged behind, unnoticed by Pontella, who continued in a slight jog towards the barn.

"Wait!"

Pontella came to an abrupt stop and turned to face her.

"Wait, Pontella," Junie repeated, softer this time. "It's right there, behind the barn."

Pontella waited for Junie to catch up to her.

"You scared?" Junie whispered into Pontella's ear when she had reached her side.

"Yeah." Pontella grabbed Junie's hand into her own. But her grip was strong, her face set in determination, as if steeling herself to see something she had been waiting for all of her young life.

The two walked side by side to the corner of the barn and stepped around it as if off a cliff. Immediately, hands grabbed at them. Junie shook her own hand from Pontella's tightening grasp and pushed her into the arms of Scoogie and the other boys.

Pontella's scream was cut short as Scoogie threw her to the ground and knocked the air out of her. Junie took a deep breath, felt a heaviness replace the air she exhaled. A dull ache spread from the bottom of her stomach into her legs as she pressed both hands into the soft flesh of her belly.

She watched as Georgie and Dennis knelt on the girl as if in prayer, their bony knees pressed into the tender flesh of her outstretched arms. Dennis's hands found their way to Pontella's mouth, and she shook her head back and forth trying to rip her face away as the hands smashed her bruised lips against her teeth. Scoogie straddled her stomach. He had ripped open her blouse, and he and Timothy now squeezed her breasts through the white training bra.

Pontella kicked her legs so that her skirt lay bunched around her waist, revealing her lavender panties. From where she stood, Junie could see the word *Saturday* embroidered in a darker purple just above the lace-edged leg hole. She looked away, and it was then that she discovered that one of the boys was missing. It was Sonny Fisher, whose small frame she now watched disappear across the field that stretched behind Mr. Alvin's land. Junie stood there until the other boys let go of Pontella and took off running after Sonny.

She looked back at the ground, feeling like she was going to be sick. Pontella had curled herself into a ball and lay on her right side, her left arm covering her breasts. Her blouse, with its Peter Pan collar, lay open. In the hush that always accompanies the coming of evening, Junie could hear the girl's quiet weeping.

Junie covered her own breasts with her arms, feeling a deep ache, one that she would not feel again until years later, when she held her child close, his mouth wet and searching.

"Junie," Pontella whispered.

Junie lowered herself to the ground and tried to help Pontella sit up, but the other girl snatched her arm away, gathered her tattered blouse around herself, and sat up on her own, then pulled her knees up to her chest.

"Why?" Pontella's voice was hoarse from crying. "Why?"

"I'm sorry, Pontella. I didn't know," Junie said, her own voice weak. She sat down beside the girl. "They said they would scare you, is all." She waited for Pontella to respond.

"It was me they really wanted. Shoulda been me," Junie mumbled. She wanted Pontella to protest, but Pontella had fixed her gaze on the field of boys, her eyes like those of a baby bird.

The two girls sat for a time in silence, their backs against the barn wall, separated by inches that seemed more like worlds, neither wanting to move from the spot because both knew that when they finally did go, they would be leaving something behind.

MORE LIKE US

Sometimes we can see her standing in front of her window, swaying to what must be music. She sways and the moonlight paints her body silver against the night sky that has settled into her, that stirs when she moves like this, rises into her breasts and into her fingertips to rain down around the room.

Hers is a moon dance, a blues song.

We heard she had grown up on a small farm somewhere a little south. A place where her days were measured by the comings and goings of the Peter-Wheat Bread truck, bottled-milk deliveries, and the weekly visit of the Charley Chip man. In between those times she waited and hoped for something to happen. Waited with a stubborn restlessness.

Even when she was doing what all the other folks were doing—going to church picnics, helping her daddy with the farming, or jitterbugging down at the hall—she gave off an air of expectancy like a perfume. She was the type to be found poised on top of a fence watching the sun go down, marking the passage of another spent day. Surely no one was surprised when her waiting moved her right on up to the city, limited her view to what she could see from the window of her one-bedroom apartment on the third floor of some brownstone where her days would end with feet swelled like a blowfish from standing all day long in a factory.

We laughed when we saw her coming with her thick-heeled shoes, her socks rolled down to the bones of her ankles, and her faded shifts, her country ways. That's what we took to calling her, Country, because of her ways. We sat on the front stoop and drank our dandelion wine while she moved through the streets of the city. We watched her get up early every morning while the sun was just a cut in the sky. The same brothers who hung on the corner doo-wopping and harmonizing took notice of her two-block trek to the bus stop each day. We watched her when she came home each night with her chin pulled turtlelike into her gray threadbare overcoat, protecting herself from the cooling nip in the air and our knowing eyes. She'd come up on us like there was something wrong in us gathering on the stoop before being driven inside by the cold. She'd nod her head as she shrank by us, pulling the bottom of her coat tight against her body, and then disappeared into the brownstone. Country thought she was too good to sit out on the stoop and drink a little dandelion wine. But we knew, we had seen her kind before, had once *been* her kind.

In the cold of winter we saw less of Country as we snuggled into the warmth of our blankets longer than usual. We were down to Sundays once she started going to that Methodist Church down on Eutaw Street. She'd materialize from the apartment around ten o'clock, the same time every Sunday, and mumble something that sounded like "G-mornin'." Acted like we were the sinners just because some of us had two or three kids by as many men. But it was her them women at the church wouldn't invite home for Sunday dinner, afraid a young, big-boned country gal like her would give their men something to think about besides ham and collard greens.

It was on her way to church that she met that nigga from down the Bottom. He was one of those conked-heads we call slick willies. She found him and figured she got what she'd been so restless for during all that waiting. Our men may not have been about much of nuthin', but most of them at least worked. And those who didn't had enough sense to pretend they had left their woman so she could get a little relief from the system. At least we didn't have us no slick willie. We could've told her all about him if she'd have asked.

Instead we saw those work boots and faded dresses give way to fitted sweaters that hung off her shoulders and emphasized her slender waist, paired with skirts that hugged her behind and open-toed slingbacks every bit of three inches high. She started walking around here like she was something new. Smiling and waving as she ran off to jazz alley down on Pennsylvania Avenue so's she could meet her willie. Wasn't long before Country stopped going to church. Too hungover to get up that early in the morning. She stopped making those weekly calls back home from the public phone in the hallway, too.

When she moved that man of hers into her flat, we never said a word. Just watched while she went to work every day, that man never leaving the house. Probably laid up in her bed waiting for her to come home with some money: those willies are lazy. She left every day and came home later and later every night, with two mouths to feed now instead of one. Even when she swelled up to where it was almost too painful for her to walk those two blocks, we never said a word.

Once the weather broke, Country's willie stopped coming home some nights. She stayed up in that one-bedroom, the sounds of Lady Day filtering through the cracks in the door while we was trying to have our rent parties. Late into the summer we heard she had had a boy. Whatever it was, it wasn't enough to keep her man from running off. Only the comings and goings of the relief worker let us know that Country was still a part of us. That and the crying every night. That baby cried like it was starving for something. Must have been colicky. After a while we got used to it. Until that one evening when all we heard was the quiet. That deep quiet, one we hadn't heard in quite some time.

Country's across-the-hall-neighbor was the one got the super to open the door. They found that girl laid up in the bed with her baby in her arms, at her breast. Dead. Somebody said it was smothered. Someone else said its head was bashed in. Said they always knew something was wrong with that girl. But people are always talking. The death was never investigated, so we never did find out. We just lived on the rumors. Babies die all the time on the Lower East Side of Baltimore. We all went to the funeral. Just pitiful. There was no one there but us and Country, and a coffin closed to eyes hungry for just one glimpse.

Now she walks past us while we sit on the stoop drinking our wine, looking like she forgot something. Looking like she forgot she had ever waited, looking more like us.

SAP RISING

Ebbie Pinder leaned against the maple the way she imagined
a movie star would: with one foot resting against the tree and
her elbows bent like wings. The cashmere sweater cupped her
breasts in a blue so delicate it appeared almost white in the
sun, its color highlighting the reddish hues in her brown skin.
She waited for Leonard, that Fisher boy whose father had
died just three months before, leaving his son everything and
making him a man in the process. It was then the two had
met. He had come to their place, along with the other men, to
help her father clear a few walnut trees. She was the one who
brought them her mother's homemade lemonade that everyone talked about. And afterwards she was the one who waited
at the gate when Leonard left to go home.

Wasn't long before he was coming that way late every afternoon. Wasn't long before she was leaving her job as upstairs maid at the Hampton place two hours early so they could meet in the orchards across from where she lived.

She looked off in the direction of Egypt Farms. They were the same orchards she had played in as a child, the same dirt road and fields she had crossed to get there. Everything the same, except now she had Leonard. He said he couldn't remember life before them, but she could. She could remember walking past her father as he worked his fields every day, on her way home from school and piano lessons. She knew that he had risen early in the morning and would stay in the fields all day, until the sun went down. And come home with an empty belly that her mother had to fill, in his sweat-soiled work clothes that chased the smell of her mother's perfume from every room. Ebbie hated that smell. Hated the sight of mud-caked boots outside the back door, waiting through the night for their owner to slip his swollen feet into them the next morning. Hated the work-stained hands that cracked and bled in the wintertime, tracing red across the bodices of her mother's dresses. Now that she had Leonard, Ebbie couldn't imagine how her mother had lasted all these years.

She squinted against the sun's glare as she gazed down the dirt road that meandered past her house and into town. She thought she caught sight of a figure off in the distance, but it turned out to be Mrs. Jarvis's fence post. It was loose, and even the slightest wind caused it to sway against the razor-thin wires that kept it from falling over. She wished the woman would fix that damn thing; it had been broken for as long as she could remember. Nothing changed here.

But Ebbie had changed. When she was a young girl, it had been just a stirring. And even then, she had tried to make it go away. She would eat food enough for a grown woman. Folks used to make fun, watching her shovel chicken and sweet potatoes and whatever else into her mouth. Waiting until she was just about done before asking her what it tasted like.

"'Taste like more," she had learned to respond, knowing they would laugh and wink and poke each other in the ribs.

They said she had a tapeworm, because no matter how much she ate, she never gained an ounce. But her mother knew. Ebbie could tell her mother knew about the wanting that slept in her belly. Knew that a time would come when no amount of food would keep it quiet.

At first, Leonard's hands on her skin, and his kisses that tasted like sun-warmed honey, had fed her. The length of his body along her own silenced the need for anything else. But lately nothing could stop it. The wanting slithered in her belly and up into her throat until she thought she would choke on it.

Ebbie pushed herself away from the tree. They had argued the night before. Leonard wanted them to tell her family and his about the two of them. Wanted to marry her. Had asked her three times already, and each time she had grown less eager. Instead, she waited. Like she had been waiting for the day when she would leave this place. She had been saving her money, every penny she earned taking her one step closer to her freedom. She couldn't count how many nights she had heard the train's whistle and dreamed of when she would be on it as it pulled out of the station.

Ebbie made her way to the Fisher place, crossing beneath the shade from the maples that lined the side of the road. She had heard stories of the city: the streets filled with garbage, a barrage of fast-moving cars, dirt-covered buildings, and people who passed one another like strangers. After the war, some town folks had moved to the city looking for work, but they had always come back home with nothing more than empty pockets and broke-down stories. Nothing worse than leaving only to come back damaged. Folks talked then. Bad enough they'd talk if she was to run in the first place. Then she'd be the one soiling the family name, leaving her mama and her sister with the task of making things right again. She raised her hand to rub the back of her neck. Best to just stay put.

When she reached the intersection of Bellona and Charles Way, Ebbie waited at the corner. Just two dirt roads, really, one ending about a half a mile on, at the woods. The creek was over there, between Moss Woods and the orchards. Ebbie had started going there on her way home from school every day. She'd race across the road and down the hill, through Egypt Farms, and into the gully that led to the creekbed. She'd throw herself at the water's edge and kneel down so her face hovered merely inches above it, trying to catch any sign that the sap was rising. Trying to see the white foam that floated on top of the surface and looked like spun sugar. And each day, nothing. Just the sounds of her shoes slapping a beat against the dust as she ran on home.

Last week she and Leonard had met in the orchards as usual. Leonard lay on the grass, his arms a pillow for his head. She sat by his side with her back against the pear tree, knees drawn up so that she could rest her chin on them. When she leaned against the bark, Ebbie could feel the sap dripping just near the shoulder of her sleeveless blouse. She wiped it off, leaning forward.

"Sap's rising." Her voice rose from her throat like butter-fly wings.

"What?"

"You know, the sap. It's rising."

"What's that mean?"

"There's an old saying—no, better than a saying; it's true. For a person who's dying. If they can just hold on long enough to see the sap rise to the surface of the water, then they'll be able to make it through the year."

"How's the sap get to the water?"

"The roots, I guess," she said, getting to her feet. "But that's not the point, Leonard." Ebbie crossed her arms in front of her chest and stepped out from under the tree's shade. Leonard rose and followed her.

"What's wrong?" he asked.

"It's the sap. Seeing the sap."

"It's just one of those Negro tales. It ain't real." He locked his arms around her waist. " 'Sides, you don't even know no-body that's ailing."

Ebbie let her head fall against his chest, shaking it back and forth, her hands balled into fists so tight her nails dug into the tender flesh of her palms. She felt the sobs gather in her chest and watched her hands fly upward, like birds, to cover her mouth and keep them from escaping. Instead she allowed Leonard to lead her back beneath the tree's branches, where she sat in near silence for the rest of the evening.

Ebbie turned in to the Fisher place, the place that would

one day be hers if she said yes. Then she would be treated like all the rest of the married women. There'd be an engagement party and then a wedding. She'd wear a simple, sleeveless tea-length dress, the color of a field of blue morning glories. She'd let Loretta twist the same flowers throughout her thick, coarse hair. And her father, who never went to church, would be able to wear his gray suit with the matching hat, and she would glide down the petal-strewn aisle on his arm, and his hands would be clean and soft.

Then, for two weeks after, the womenfolk would come by with plates: Mrs. Francis's potato salad, Mrs. Aileen's catfish, and Mrs. Roberta's peach cobbler. And her mama's home-squeezed lemonade. She wouldn't have to do nothing except take care of Leonard. The only time she'd leave the bed would be to make a plate of food for her husband. She did like the sound of that word.

Ebbie had never come here to look for him. She could see that the house had been freshly painted, white set against blue trim and window sashes. Blue was her favorite color. She could see the car in the garage. He was home. She made her way into the yard, where farm equipment littered the area like oversized playthings left unattended. Some had started to rust.

Ebbie was about to knock on the screen door when a movement caught her eye, turned her head, and off in the distance she could see someone. It took her a few moments to realize it was Leonard.

He wore what looked like a brown work hat pulled down tight on his head. He was driving the tractor, the monotonous drone of the engine filling the air. Ebbie knew he would never be able to hear her if she called out to him. Instead she stood riveted by the sight of that man riding back and forth, back and forth, through row after row of corn stubble, realizing that no matter how long she stood there, he would never look up. She slumped against the door, suddenly worn down.

Reluctantly, she turned to go. As she was leaving the Fisher yard, she looked back over her shoulder and saw that Leonard was still in the same position, hunched over the wheel of his tractor, moving mindlessly through his fields. He would never know she had been there. Ebbie made her way back down the road. The farther away she got, the faster she walked, until she found herself running. She ran until it felt like she couldn't breathe. Ran until the clouds of dust kicked up by her feet made her disappear.

That night, while Leonard waited in the orchard, too tired to notice the intoxicating scent of ripening fruit, Ebbie made her way through the darkness. There were no street lights, just the moon to navigate her way, the sway of her hips, like a ship crossing the ocean, taking her closer to where the train's whistle sang her lament.

WINTER'S WHEAT

The deer seemed to fold into itself, wilted onto the cold, unyielding earth at the edge of the road. Its lids closed on eyes resigned to the inevitability of death as the car passed by in a whisper. But for the headlights casting a halo into the blackness, capturing the wounded animal in their glow, Boag Mason would have sworn he'd made the whole thing up.

He looked at his father and mother in the front seat, hoping to find some hint that they recognized the deer's plight, too. His father's gaze never once left the road ahead. But there was something in the way his mother placed the tips of her fingers and rested her forehead against the icy glass of the passenger window that made Boag think he was not the only one who had seen.

He was about to ask her when he caught a movement out of the corner of his eye. He slid across the backseat to press his face against the window and peered into the darkness, where he could just make out the tiny figure of a baby deer as it zigzagged toward the car. He held his breath, thinking the frightened creature would run straight into them, but at the last minute the orphan turned and leapt into the cornfield, disappeared into the night. His father never saw a thing.

Boag fell back hard against the leather seat. Every few seconds he kept turning to look out of the rear window.

"What's wrong, son?" Mr. Mason asked.

"Sir, did you see the deer back there?"

"Back where?"

" 'Bout a mile back." Boag motioned with his thumb.

"Can't say's I did."

"It was on the side of the road."

"Well, this the season, son. You likely to see all kinds of deer right about now."

"Not like this one."

His father glanced over his shoulder. "And what made this one so different?"

"This one looked like . . ." Boag leaned forward. "Like she was human or somethin'."

His father's laughter rumbled throughout the car. "So the deer wasn't really a deer at all, eh?"

Boag ducked back into his seat, grateful for the darkness that hid his reddening face.

"Leave the boy be, Franklin," his mother scolded.

He knew he had an imagination; he had often gotten in trouble because of it. But that was when he was a child. He'd just turned thirteen, and it was time for him to put away childish things. Time his parents let him. He closed his eyes and tried to ignore the soft laughter that came from the front seat. Tried to let the hum of the car's wheels on the country road erase all thoughts of injured deer with human souls.

His father turned in to the driveway and brought the car to a standstill beside the modest farmhouse so Boag and his mother wouldn't stain their Sunday shoes walking from the garage in the dark. As soon as the car had stopped, Boag leapt out and headed for the back porch.

"Boag," his mother called after him.

"Sorry, Mama." He hurried back to where his mother waited with her door open, took the hand she extended, and gently guided her to her feet.

"A gentleman always helps a lady in and out of a car."

"Yes, Mama."

He took his place beside his mother as they stepped onto the carpet of grass, already beginning to soften with night dew. He held her bony elbow in his still-childlike hand and led her to the bottom of the porch steps. Without waiting for his mother's instructions, Boag bounded to the top and yanked on the screen door until it flew open. His mother passed through unobstructed.

Once on the porch, Boag went to stand by the back door while his mother retrieved the spare key from under the wicker laundry basket in the corner. He would have gotten the key for her, but he was forbidden to touch it—just another reminder of how his parents continued to see him as a child. He told himself it didn't matter as he tossed back his head to blow breath rings toward the porch's ceiling.

"Cold, Boag?" his mother asked when she joined him.

"Just smokin' my pipe."

Mrs. Mason laughed as she unlocked the door. She stepped to the side and waited for him to notice. At first Boag thought to pretend like he didn't see his mother. He didn't want to be a gentleman anymore. He wanted to be a pirate like the ones he saw at the picture shows on Saturdays, that or a farmer like his father. And he was sure a pirate would never open a door for a girl, even if the girl was his own mother. But Boag knew her. Knew that she would stand there waiting, would bring him into some delicate test of wills he didn't fully understand, but one she usually seemed to win. And besides, he was cold. He reached over and opened the door.

"Hey, Mama?"

"Mmm?" His mother looked at him as he came to stand in the center of the kitchen.

"You saw that deer."

Mrs. Mason turned her back without answering.

"Mama?" Boag persisted. "There was somethin' about that deer—"

"Whew, it's cold!" Boag's father thundered as he bustled into the room.

Mr. Mason was a big, gentle man whose face crinkled at the eyes with unchecked laughter. He was the one who had given Boag the nickname Chucks—short for Chuckles—as a young child, their shared amusements being one of the few markings of a bond between a little boy and his father.

Now, wrapped in his caramel-colored wool overcoat, he

looked to Boag like nothing so much as a ferocious bear. Boag laughed at the idea as he watched his father shake off the chill air that clung to him.

"That's enough, Franklin," his mother admonished, her voice suddenly small and tight.

"Wha'd I do?" Boag's father stared at his wife until she looked away.

"Boag, you go on up. Get yourself ready for bed."

"Yes, ma'am."

He wiped the smile from his face and tried not to look at either of his parents as he headed for the stairs. He couldn't help feeling like he had become the prize calf in some silent auction. And where before he would have used that to his advantage, at that moment all he wanted was for his parents to be like they used to, when his love could find no difference between the two.

"And don't forget to wash your feet. I don't want my sheets dirtied."

"Yes, Mama."

"I'll be up in a minute."

"OK, Mama."

He wished his mother would stop treating him like he was still five years old. Tucking him into bed. He was probably the only boy his age in Grandville whose mother still came to him each night. She wouldn't even let his uncle Jimmy take him hunting, though every other boy thirteen or younger had been doing so for years.

Boag switched on his light and made his way into his cluttered bedroom, a space dominated by the bookcases, desk, and telescope that his mother believed every potential scholar should own. He shrugged off his rumpled suit jacket and tossed it at the bed, missing the footboard by inches. Next came the dress shirt and pants; he let them fall in a heap in the middle of the floor. His mother would take care of everything when she came to say good night, he thought as he ignored the washstand with its pitcher and basin and went over to the bookcase closest to the window.

His hunting knife was hidden there, the one his uncle Jimmy had given him for his birthday four months ago. When he first held the black leather case in his hands, Boag hoped his mother would finally allow him to join his uncles on their next hunting trip. Instead, he had never seen her so angry as when he showed her the knife. For days after, she bombarded him while he studied at the kitchen table, going on about her disdain for men who slaughtered defenseless animals, the guilt they should feel, how they would one day have to stand before God and answer for their transgressions. And then, after a week of subjecting him to all of that and even a few tears, she shocked him by declaring that it was his choice whether or not he wanted to keep such a horrid thing. "And I know you'll make the right one," she added as she left him to deal with his conflicting emotions.

Boag reached behind a set of books and pulled out the sequestered knife. He checked to see if the blade needed to be cleaned and sharpened, as he had done every other day since his uncle gave it to him. After seeing those deer, he didn't think he'd ever have the nerve to use the thing. Boag had just started to put the knife back in its place when he heard his mother's footsteps on the stairs. He quickly straightened the bookcase and hurried over to the bed.

"Ready for me?" his mother asked as she entered the room.

"Yes, ma'am." Boag yawned as he opened the covers and slid between crisp, cool sheets.

"You wash your feet?"

"Uh-huh."

His mother stooped to pick up his discarded clothing before going to the closet, her back to the bed. He prayed she wouldn't stop to see if there was any water in the basin.

"Mama?"

"Yes."

"That deer."

His mother turned to face him. "Boag, why you going on about a deer?"

He waited until she had finished hanging the clothes and come to sit down on the edge of his bed, her diminutive figure barely making an impression on the mattress. Then he asked, "But you saw it?"

"I saw it."

"At first she tried to stand, but then she just sorta gave in. Like she decided to die."

His mother placed her hand on his chest. "Boag, honey, I don't usually agree with your father, but it was just a deer."

"But her eyes." He tried to pin down his mother's eyes with his own.

"What about them?"

"So helpless and sad."

"Well, it's over now."

"But what about the baby?"

"What baby?" His mother frowned.

"There was another deer, a baby. She had a baby. That's what made her eyes so sad, I think."

Mrs. Mason stared out the bedroom window. "Sometimes things happen we can't explain, Boag." She looked down at her son. "Just get some rest, OK?"

His mother bent forward and placed on his lips a kiss so light he wasn't sure she had kissed him at all. "That's why this thing is getting to you: you're tired, is all." She tucked the covers under his chin and stood to leave.

"Mama?"

"Yes, son?"

"What do you think happened to him? The baby."

"Boag, please."

"I just want to know," he begged.

"That baby's probably dead by now. A child can't make it in the wild without its mother, everybody knows that!" His mother moved away from the bed, the heels of her pumps striking the hardwood floor as she made her way to the door. Once there, she turned back to look at him, her voice suddenly a soft caress.

"Good night, son," his mother whispered. "And Boag, you don't have to worry, Mama's not going anywhere."

She switched off the light and withdrew from the room, leaving him alone in the darkness to find sleep around the burden of knowing too much yet being helpless to do anything about it.

The next morning Boag awakened before the sun had had a chance to chase away the shadows, which looked like fallen animals in the corners of his room. By the time he got dressed in his work clothes and went down to the kitchen, his mother had already cleared his father's dishes.

"Mornin', Mama." Boag threw himself onto his chair. He loaded his plate with eggs and scrapple from the platter in the center of the table without waiting for his mother to do it for him.

"Good morning. You up early." She came over to where he sat, looked down at the food that had just missed his plate.

"Mm-hmm."

"Something going on in school today?"

"I dunno," he answered around the food in his mouth. "I'm not goin' to school this week. Gotta help Papa with the fields, remember?"

"Is that right?" His mother raised her eyebrow.

"Yes, ma'am. Papa said I could."

"Well, ask *me* if you can."

Boag looked at his mother.

"I'll tell you. The answer's no."

"But Mama!"

"You heard me. I said no."

He knew there was no use trying to talk to her about anything that had to do with him missing school. That was a sore subject between his mother and father. Mrs. Mason, a college-educated woman, wanted her son to have the opportunity to become anything other than a farmer, even if that was the only thing he really wanted.

"Ain't fair," he mumbled.

" '*Isn't* fair.' " She sat down next to him. "And don't talk to me about fair. Is it fair that I've worked hard to make sure you have a decent life, only to have my efforts thrown back in my face? Is *that* fair?"

Boag looked down at his plate.

"Well, son, is that fair to me?" Her voice cracked, and Boag looked up to see tears in his mother's eyes.

"No, Mama."

"No, it's not. Now, we won't have to go through this anymore, will we? Talk of working in fields, dirty hands and . . ." Her voice trailed off.

"No, ma'am."

"Good. Now go on and eat and get ready for school. Mama has to get this kitchen cleaned so she can get her hair done." She got up from the table, assured that the matter was over.

After Boag had finished his breakfast and changed from his work clothes into an outfit more suitable for school, he made his way from the house down to the fields where he knew his father waited.

He did feel sorry for his mother, he acknowledged as he passed the barn. He knew how much she had sacrificed for him. All his life he had been hearing the stories about how his mother and his uncle Jimmy and Jimmy's wife, Alvine, had once belonged to a singing group known as The Grands.

He heard how they had traveled around to different towns performing in churches and halls, both spiritual and secular music. Folks said his mother had a voice that could bring the most coldhearted of sinners to their knees.

That's how she had met his father, through his younger brother, Jimmy. Franklin Mason, a man almost twice her age—whose first wife had died trying to give her husband a baby—had fallen in love with the woman whose voice made grown men cry. Six tries before he finally convinced her to become his second wife, a farmer's wife. His father's second choice. From his days of playing ball, Boag knew what it felt like to be the last one chosen. But for a woman like his mother to live that way every day of her life, well, he couldn't imagine how she could take it.

Once Boag was born, he became her world, her whole reason for living. Nothing else mattered to her. By then she had stopped singing altogether, had lost her voice.

Boag could see his father standing in the field talking with the two hands he had hired to help him. His father spoke in a loud, coarse tone, one that Boag had never heard before and that stopped him in his tracks. He lingered under the willow in what was still considered to be the Masons' backyard until he caught his father's eye. His father came over to where Boag waited with his schoolbooks and lunch bucket.

"Mornin', son."

Boag looked at his father's smiling face, his own eyes tight with anger. "Why'n't you stand up for me?" he blurted before he could stop himself.

"What're you talkin' 'bout, Boag?"

"Mama. Why'n't you tell her I was workin' with you this week?"

"Boag."

"No, Papa."

His father looked down at the ground. "I was goin' to, son. I really was. Guess it just slipped my mind."

"Well, she said no. Said I had to go to school."

"I'm sorry." His father shrugged his shoulders, then spread his hands as if to show his son just how empty they were.

Boag knew that feeling of not being able to do anything about a given situation, but that his father felt that way only angered him even more. Abruptly, he stepped out from the cover of the willow tree and headed across the grass.

"It's gon' be all right, Chucks," his father yelled at Boag's retreating back. Boag ignored him, already distracted by what he imagined awaited him at school.

When he reached the road, Boag thought about all the other boys working side by side with their fathers during the next few weeks of harvest, planting crops of winter's wheat that would last through the harshest of seasons. That would grow golden and tall in spite of weather cold enough to kill any seed too weak to stand against it. So filled with purpose only the deer could threaten the resolute crops' chances at life.

At the rate he was going, he would never have the opportunity to know what it meant to work the land, would never know the father who talked like a hired hand, never come to understand him in the way only two men working a field together could get to know each other. Boag was condemned to sit in a classroom in which the only boys left were those too young to be of any use farming anyway. Babies. And him.

He passed by the Fuller place, where he could make out the figures of Hiron and Mr. Fuller in their field, the younger Fuller already as tall as his father. Boag didn't even try to avoid being seen by them. There was no use. By the end of the day everyone would know how his mother wouldn't let him stay home. He'd rather die than go to school, a feeling he hadn't had since third grade, when his mother refused to buy him his first pair of long pants. She kept him in knickers well after everyone else. Even after he came home from school bruised and sometimes beaten from the battles he fought each day, his mother could not be swayed. It wasn't until he took matters into his own hands that things changed.

He remembered stealing away to Moss Woods every afternoon, hiding in the cover of trees while he pulled off his knickers. The ache in his small hands and shoulders as he struggled to separate the material that threatened to keep him bound. And how every night his mother would frustrate his efforts by repairing each tear. The two went back and forth like that for weeks until she surprised him by giving in one day, sent him and his father to Mr. Haddaway's to buy his first real pair of trousers. He never forgot how grown up he felt having pants, and how frightened he was to learn his mother could be so easily defeated.

Boag reached the narrow road aptly named Schoolyard Lane just as the smaller children were arriving. Their glances seemed an accusation as they skipped by him to the one-room schoolhouse nestled at the end of the path. A congregation of children had already gathered around, awaiting the bell that would tell them it was time to begin their day. But Boag couldn't bring himself to follow them in all their cheerful, childish blindness.

Instead he turned and headed back in the direction he had come from. He knew only that he could not stomach the thought of sitting in the rear of the classroom, alone and left behind. Nor could he go down to the woods and wait until it was time for school to let out; it was too damp and cold for that.

He crossed the two dirt roads that marked Grandville's main intersection, praying that no one's mother or father would see him as he made his way to the westernmost end of the Mason property, the side that faced the Fullers' place. That way he could sneak back unseen, letting the house block his approach from his father's view in the fields.

Boag stood on top of the slight incline of land that overlooked the farmhouse and the now-empty garage and realized his mother had left to get her hair done. And before he could talk himself out of what he was about to do, he ran at full speed for the garage, which was really nothing more than a shack of weathered planks. He hid his books and lunch in the mulberry bushes and pulled his bike free from the dark, musty shed. He pushed the bicycle into the front yard, all the while checking to make sure his father hadn't come around the side of the house. Once he had cleared the end of the driveway, Boag jumped on his bike and took off for Ariel, the next town over from Grandville. He needed to see his uncle Jimmy, who owned a hardware store there. Boag would tell his uncle about this mess with his parents and the deer, and his uncle would tell him how a person could wake up one day and find his whole world somehow changed.

He had never defied his parents so openly. And none of the other boys had ever dared, either. Boag saw a car at the end of Charles Way; his stomach skipped in fear of his being seen. He couldn't afford for that to happen, because then his parents would know all about his adventure even before he could make it back home: word spread like seeds on a strong wind in a place like Grandville. So he kept his eyes trained on the path ahead and behind. Anytime he saw anything that resembled a car or truck, he jumped off his bike and crouched within the thicket of bushes and rows of cornfields that lined the edge of the road.

Boag made the whole trip like this, stopping every few minutes, too, to hide from maples that looked like scrawny Mrs. Fisher or clumps of shrubbery that reminded him of old man Pinder. At other times he found himself searching the distant trees for signs of a lone baby deer. By the time he finally reached Ariel, he was covered with dirt and bits of leaves, and his nerves were wound so tight his body ached with the effort of holding everything in.

Ariel was just like any other small, one-road town, except to a boy on a solitary and forbidden journey. He had never been anyplace significant without his parents, let alone in a whole other town, he thought as he pedaled mercilessly down the main thoroughfare to his uncle's store. He looked around at unfamiliar faces and found that the sliver of fear that had earlier settled in the pit of his stomach had now been replaced by what he could only call a feeling of being set loose—like Miss Alberta when she got the Holy Ghost in church each Sunday. It brought a smile to his face.

His uncle Jimmy's hardware store stood at the end of a block-long row of businesses. Boag rode past a bakery and a general store with a headless mannequin in the window. He parked his bike near the corner and peered into the storefront window. He couldn't see anyone moving around inside, but the sign on the door said "Open," scribbled in his uncle's own hand, so Boag grabbed the handle and walked in. The makeshift chimes—three small, tarnished Christmas bells on orange yarn—sounded his arrival. Seconds later, his uncle appeared from the back room.

He wore black trousers, a white dress shirt, and a black waistcoat. And with his wire-rimmed glasses perched on the edge of his nose, he looked more like a teacher than a man who ran a store filled with hammers and saws.

"Hey, Uncle Jimmy!" Boag flicked his wrist in a wave, try-ing to appear as if his uncle was used to seeing him in town alone in the middle of the day.

"Boy, what the hell you doin' over here? Is everythin' all right at home?"

Boag loved it when his uncle cussed around him; he was the only adult who treated him as if he wasn't too young to hear that kind of language. "Nobody's in trouble, if that's what you mean to ask."

"Well, fine. You can take your butt right on back home, then."

"But I need to talk to you about somethin'."

"This ain't a good time right now. I was just comin' out here to lock the door."

"But it's important." Boag went to stand next to his uncle.

"What's wrong, son?"

"Uncle Jimmy, you think deer have a soul?"

"Whew." His uncle sat down on the stool behind the counter. "That's a question for God."

Boag nodded solemnly, satisfied with his uncle's response. He knew he'd made the right choice in coming here. His uncle would never laugh at him or tell him he was too tired or too young to understand.

"Last night I saw a deer. And I would swear on a stack of Bibles she had a soul. Like she was human. And ever since then I'm thinkin' I could never be a hunter." He took a deep breath and looked at his uncle.

"Go on, I'm listenin'."

"I looked at that knife you gave me—"

"I thought your mama made you get rid of that thing?"

Boag frowned at his uncle. "Who told you that?"

"Never mind. Just go on with what you was sayin'."

"I looked at that huntin' knife and it's like everythin' is changin'."

"But that ain't a bad thing, Boag."

"Yeah, but then this mornin' Mama wouldn't let me stay home and work the fields with Papa. She wants me to be a businessman like you, but all I really want to be is a farmer like Papa. And I don't think her reasons have anything to do with me at all. The truth is, I'm just sick to death of my parents." When he was done, Boag sagged against the counter. There, he'd said it.

He watched as his uncle crossed his arms over his broad chest. "Is that what's got you so riled up? You don't have a thing to worry about."

"Did you hear me say I'm sick of my parents?"

"I heard you." His uncle laughed. "Look, maybe it ain't them that's changin', maybe it's you. And that's all right, Boag."

Boag turned and looked out the store window. What his uncle said was true: he *was* changing, had started to change the way he looked at everything around him.

"Look, my lunch date's been sittin' in the back room all this time," Uncle Jimmy said. "Let me go tell I'll be a while longer and you and me'll go get a grape pop. And then you'll get on back home, how's that sound?"

Boag looked back at his uncle and nodded his head. "Sounds fine."

His uncle got up from the stool and went over to the curtain that separated the front from the back of the store.

"Uncle Jimmy?"

"Yeah?"

"Why do people hunt, anyway?"

"Well, look at it thisaway. Sometimes somethin' gots to die in order for somethin' else to live. It's like the law of the land. Ain't no room for feelin' sorry when you the one tryin' to live." His uncle turned and disappeared behind the cotton drapes.

"About that knife," Boag yelled to his uncle, and when he

didn't receive an answer, he moved closer to the other side of the store. He couldn't help himself: he leaned forward and peered into the back room through a slit in the curtains, his eyes adjusting to the gloom.

He watched as his uncle knelt down in front of the loveseat. Boag could just about make out the silhouette of a woman. And he knew it wasn't his aunt Alvine. The two grown-ups spoke to each other in whispers. Boag wanted his uncle to hurry and take him for a pop like he'd said.

"Uncle Jimmy?" Boag squeaked, his throat suddenly dry.

He stood riveted to the spot even though he wanted to turn away, watched as the woman raised her hand and touched the tips of her fingers to his uncle's lips. Boag's eyes squinted. He felt himself grow so hot he thought he would faint.

He didn't remember running from the store in desperation. But the next thing he knew, he was at the corner, crouched against the brick wall. He buried his face in his hands and tried to erase the image of his mother hidden in the shadows of his uncle's back room. He stayed that way until he heard the all-too-familiar sound of high heels as his mother came to stand before him.

"Boag?"

He ignored her, waited for her to say something that would make it all better.

"Boag, don't tell your father. You'd kill him if you did."

He jumped to his feet as if she had kicked him, a chill anger steeling his shoulders as he pulled himself to his full height. He looked into his mother's face, and her eyes were the first to turn away.

"I gotta go help Papa with the winter's wheat." Boag grabbed his bike and took off at a run, leaving his mother standing at the edge of the road. When he had picked up enough speed, he hopped on the seat and pedaled with all of his might, until he had stirred up the wind enough to wipe the tears from his face.

"Ain't no room for feelin' sorry when you the one tryin' to live": his uncle's words echoed in Boag's head as he made his way back to where he knew his father would be.

WISHES

When Cynthia Mae Fuller was six years old, she changed her name to Cinnamon. Went through a different name every other week or so before finally deciding. Refused to answer to anything but that or Cinny. Ma'D kept on calling her by the name she gave her after all that hard laboring, until they both got worn down and Ma'D just gave in.

"Cynthia too sweet a name for a gal like you anyhow," Ma'D said.

Cinny shrugged her shoulders, but her face balled up like a big old fist. That child was powerful rough, like gravel scraping soft feet. She was always scraping and scratching. She was the one her sisters, Hira, Cease, and Tavi, ran to whenever someone teased them to tears or threatened to do them harm.

She was dark like the stained wood of a Tupelo tree, with skin as smooth as river stones. She had thick, wavy hair, black as oil and just as shiny, kept in two braids on either side of her head that flowed down to the top of her back. But it was Cinny's eyes that held a person. Not only because of how those long lashes curled around her dark brown eyes, but because of the way she would look at a person. Ma'D said it was disrespectful the way that child looked at grown folks. Would beat Cinny something awful sometimes, trying to "knock the snuff out of her," as Ma'D used to say.

Folks blamed her daddy, Hiron Fuller, for the way that child turned out, and it was his fault, really. She was the one who cleaned up after him when he came home drunk, after Ma'D refused to do it anymore. She was the one knew all the secrets of a grown man's frailties. And her only a child.

That's what led to her making that wish. She would never forget the first time she made it. It was the last time the two of them had gone fishing. She had been perched on the edge of the creek all morning listening to her daddy going on about Ma'D and the war, until his words slid into a hum and a picture began to form in her mind's eye of him facedown in the waist-high waters, his arms outstretched and head hanging down like he was nailed to the cross. At first Cinny tried to make it go away, but she couldn't. Even after they came home with that day's catch, sitting on the back porch with scales flying. Even as she pulled the sharpened knife through the trout's fat belly and scooped its guts out with her bare hands, that picture of her daddy still filled her head. Cinny added it to her prayers that night and each night afterward. Right at the end, just a whisper asking God to make it so her daddy would go away. And when he didn't come home for a few days, she almost believed God had heard.

That was the same summer Cinny and Miss Neeva's nephew, Inch, became best friends. They made an odd pair, Cinny and the scrawny, bucktoothed boy who'd rather play jump rope with the girls instead of baseball with the rest of the town boys and Cinny. Inch was the only one called Cinny by the name Cinnamon. He wasn't a real townie. He lived in the city and only came up to stay with his two aunts, who had a place across the railroad tracks, down by the whistle stop, every spring and summer vacation. And even though Inch had been coming every year for the past three years, he was still considered nothing more than a visitor—that is, until he did something no other child had ever dared do, which was mess with Cinny.

His real name was Claymont, after his momma's last name before she married his daddy, but all the kids called him Inch on account of someone dared him to pull one of Cinny's braids one day and he did. You wouldn't know it by looking at her, but Cinny could beat up every child in town—boys, too. Cinny could run faster, climb higher, was strong. Well, Inch did it and took off running soon as he done it. Down the dirt road toward Moss Woods with Cinny chasing after. Inch was little, low to the ground, and so he outran Cinny for a good little ways. Wasn't until he was out of breath that he pushed his back up against a walnut tree and whimpered for Cinny not to kill him dead. Said the only reason he done it was because he wanted to touch her hair. Cinny towered over him for a few minutes to scare him real good before saying,

"What I look like beatin' you up? You ain't no bigger'n an inch." When the other children heard Inch telling what had happened, they took to calling him that. But he didn't mind at all. From then on, everywhere you looked, there went Cinny and Inch.

Anyhow, that was the summer Cinny said it out loud, and Inch was the one she told it to. Cinny and Inch went off one evening, him following behind that girl. Made their way down Bellona Avenue, into the orchards and over to the creek. Cinny sat down on one of the tree logs that had fallen during some forgotten storm and started to remove her jeans. Inch came and sat down beside her. Unlike Cinny, he wore shoes and socks even during the summertime, and so he bent over to undo his shoelaces.

"Cinnamon?"

"What?"

"What would you have done to me if I hadn't been too short?"

"You don't want to know." She laughed and pulled off her T-shirt so that all she had on was her underpants. Then she ran and splashed into the cool water.

"Ahh!" she screamed. "It's cold."

Inch, who had started taking off his own pants, hesitated. "Maybe I'll just sit here and watch you swim."

"You better get your butt in this water, Inch."

"Or what?" He giggled.

"Or I'ma come out there and drag you in, clothes and all!"

"My aunts would kill me dead," he said, unbuttoning his slacks and pulling off his shirt. "Hang on, I'm coming."

Inch waded into the creek slowly, rubbing at the goose-bumps that raised up on his arms and across his birdlike chest. Cinny dipped her head beneath the surface and swam behind him.

"Cinnamon?" He fluttered both hands in the water in a circle around him. "Cin?"

Suddenly his feet flew out from under him and he sank down to the bottom, Cinny's hand tight around his ankle.

Inch sputtered as he popped his head out of the water. "Cinnamon!" He wiped the water from his eyes so he could see the laughing girl who stood in front of him. "You trying to drown me?" Inch pushed a wave of water toward her. "Trying to kill me dead?"

Cinny's face darkened. She swam away from him and over to the creekbed. She left the water and fell down in the dirt.

Inch followed. "What's wrong, Cinnamon?"

"Nuthin'." She pulled her knees up to her chin.

"I know you. Something's wrong."

"If I tell you, you gotta promise not to tell nobody."

Inch threw himself down next to her, his face shiny and eager. "Cross my heart, hope to die, you can spit right in my eye," he said, making an X over his heart and holding his eye stretched wide in case Cinny wanted to spit in it. "Now, what is it, Cin?"

Cinny started telling Inch about her wish. How her daddy got on her nerves, how she hated him. How she wished he was dead sometimes. She looked at Inch, holding her breath, waiting for him to say how awful a person she was. But Inch only laughed his horsey laugh and told Cinny how he sometimes imagined his own daddy being hit by the streetcar he took home from work.

"You don't think I'm going to hell?"

"Naw."

"Think I'm evil?"

Inch laughed. "You evil and nasty and mean as a polecat!"

Cinny laughed, too, though she was still worried. She knew there were some things that could send a child to hell.

It wasn't until the next spring that several of the town's men finally did knock on the door with news about Hiron Fuller, and by then Cinny had nearly forgotten those prayers she had prayed all summer long. They'd found her daddy on the other side of Moss Woods, where he had been finishing a job for one of the white men in town. Ma'D told Cinny and her sisters that evening, leaving Cinny feeling giddy from knowing. She felt like climbing the tallest tree she could find until she reached the tiniest branches at the very tip, then clinging on while the wind whipped her from side to side. Felt like running until her sides ached and she wanted to throw up.

Instead she stayed near home, sat out on the back porch with her sisters all that day and the next while grown folks came in and out, visiting with Ma'D. Miss Neeva and her sister came near about suppertime of the second day with Inch in tow. He had just come up the night before on spring vacation. Inch joined Cinny and the other three girls out on the porch. The five children sat in near-perfect silence, only the creaking of the porch swing keeping time. Inch asked Cinny if she wanted to go on down to Egypt Farms and sit awhile, noticing how she hadn't said a word to him all evening. Cinny shook her head no, not able to look him in the face. She couldn't say how she didn't want to go to the place where she had spoken those words out loud. She knew somehow that the trees still held all her secrets, was afraid they would whisper them back as the wind shook loose their leaves. Cinny waited for Inch's aunts to finish their business and go on home, taking their nephew with them.

Cinny started doing most everything Ma'D wanted her to do, nothing like before. She stayed home, helped Ma'D with the chores. Like it was time to settle up again. Wasn't until that first Sunday after the funeral that Ma'D and Cinny argued again.

The sun woke Cinny that morning, its rays spread across the bed where she lay, bathing her in the heat of its pure light. Birds chirped like it was a regular spring morning, and for a minute Cinny forgot about the dreams that had haunted her sleep for the past week, the past four years. Ma'D had let her sleep late while the other three girls had their breakfast, and Cinny felt rested as she bounded on naked feet into the bathroom, with nothing on but her favorite pair of bloomers, the ones Ma'D hated. The elastic had come loose in both leg holes, making them flap against her thighs whenever she moved.

The pink and white bathroom had once been Cinny's favorite room in the house. It was decorated with lace curtains the same shade of pink as the inside of a conch shell. A rug hugged the base of the toilet, and a hand-woven floor mat—

one that Ma'D had made out of old dresses the girls couldn't fit into anymore—lay in front of the sink, all different shades of pink.

The room reminded Cinny of the sweet taste of a peppermint stick. It was a girl's room. A girl sweet and good. Cinny looked around her, and it was at that moment she decided she wasn't going to church.

She got up from the toilet to brush her teeth and wash her face. She took her time with her grooming this morning, where usually she just rushed right through. She wanted to stay in that bathroom all day. Sit there for hours and do nothing but look out of the tiny window at the leaves that brushed the side of their farmhouse when the wind blew, and the bluest of sky just beyond that.

But she would be forced to leave soon enough. Cinny knew Ma'D wanted all her girls to go to church, dressed in their Sunday best, like doll babies. And especially Cinny, because she was the prettiest of all the Fuller girls.

Any other time, Cinny would've gone on along with Ma'D, fit herself with clothes that never seemed quite right for her. She said they made her itch. You'd see her by the end of service rumpled, her socks sagging down her legs like melted ice cream running down into her dusty shoes. Cinny opened the bathroom door and walked past the room Cease and Tavi shared to where she slept with her sister Hira. Ma'D was in her own bedroom fixing her hair. Cinny could see that Ma'D had already laid out her outfit along with Hira's.

She sat down on her bed and crossed her arms over her flat chest, her face set. She was tired of everyone else living their lives through her. This was it. Cinny could feel a strange power building up inside as she heard Ma'D getting ready. Her head felt like it would explode with all its secrets, and she wondered if this was what it felt like to be free.

When Ma'D came into her room and told her to go on and get dressed, Cinny said she wasn't going to church no more. Looked her mother straight in the eyes and said no.

"Yes, you goin'," Ma'D said, paying no attention to her daughter.

But Cinny just clamped her lips shut even tighter and stared at the wall. She could see anger spreading over her mother's face, making her look like she was someone else. All the anger that woman had been holding on to for years.

"Uh-huh, keep on. I'm going to fan your tail for you real good. You think you grown?" Ma'D hollered.

"Humph." Cinny rolled her eyes up in her head and flattened her lips, daring Ma'D to strike her. And she did, she jumped on Cinny so fast, hollering and fussing, just kept on hitting her and saying, "You think you grown? Huh? You think you a woman?"

Usually Ma'D used a switch, which the children had to get from a tree out in the yard, but for Cinny she would use almost anything. This time she grabbed a leather shoe, the closest thing. Cinny's sisters ran upstairs soon as they heard Ma'D yelling, knowing what was coming next, scared half to death. They huddled in the doorway of the room, Tavi with both hands over her ears, whimpering, praying for Cinny to go on and cry so Ma'D would stop. But Cinny didn't utter a sound. Tears welled up in her eyes until she couldn't see a thing, but she clamped her lips down on the sobs that threatened to escape.

She felt like she was being baptized, felt like she was being absolved, though she didn't know that was what it was called. She felt like she was getting her mother's and God's forgiveness, each smack of the leather against her bare skin silencing the leaves that whispered inside her head. Ma'D must've realized something strange was going on, because she stopped hitting Cinny long enough to start hollering again.

"I don't have time for your mess," Ma'D screamed, her chest heaving. Getting only Cinny's stare in response.

She threw the shoe onto the floor and hustled the other girls to get dressed and out the door, pretending like they was late, leaving Cinny sitting on her bed, naked and bruised.

Ma'D and her girls trudged on to church in their Sunday best, Ma'D wearing her mourning like it was the only thing that could save her. Cinny's sisters were dressed in lemon and light sky-blue with shiny black patent-leather shoes and slicked-down pigtails. Their hands linked them together like a string of cutout paper dolls.

And Cinny, dirty as a polecat, marched like a general down the road, because as soon as Ma'D had shut the door, she'd thrown on her dirty coveralls and started off toward the railroad tracks and Miss Neeva's, feet stomping up clods of dust, pigtails slapping a rhythm across her back where only moments before the sting of Ma'D's whupping had broken the skin. As Ma'D and her girls entered the churchyard where the women always gathered, a bouquet of flowered dresses and hats, and the men swapped lies and smoked the last of their home-rolled cigarettes before having to sit through three hours of service, Cinny was banging on Miss Neeva's back door calling for Inch to come on outside. Miss Neeva didn't believe in going to church every single Sunday, which was a good thing for the boy, who hated sitting through the drawn-out services.

Inch ran down the porch steps to where Cinny stood digging her toe into the dirt. "What's goin' on, Cinnamon?" he asked.

"Let's go." Cinny grabbed Inch by the arm and they took off racing, not stopping until they reached the cool shade of the orchards. Both out of breath, they threw themselves on their backs into the wetness of the morning grass. The leaves murmured overhead as the wind disturbed them. Cinny closed her eyes to see if she could catch the secrets they told: nothing.

"Cinnamon."

"Inch, my name's Cynthia Mae Fuller now."

"Wha'?"

"You heard me."

"I declare, Cinny, keeping up with you is like trying to hold on to smoke . . . or wishes."

LAST WILL

June looked at the papers in her lap with something close to fear. Her father had placed the weighty brown envelope in her hands earlier that afternoon, after the funeral, when the town folks were crowded into the tiny farmhouse for the repast. She'd stuck the packet of papers into the outside pocket of her carryall bag, where it had stayed until after she took her seat on the train and settled in for the ride back to college.

Now she had in her possession what looked like some story written in her grandmother's tidy handwriting, but she was too afraid to do anything except gape at it in confusion. She couldn't understand why Grandma Mason had given this to her; she'd hardly known the woman, the relationship between June's father and his mother so strained that as the years passed, the only times June had seen her were Christmas and Mother's Day. But she had heard the stories about her grandmother, all the tales she needed to hear in a small town that passed down its secrets like treasured heirlooms.

June looked out the window. The sun was just beginning to dip below the trees, turning the sky a fiery orange and dusky purple. To June it was a joyous response, the sky's transformation, a welcome embrace for a wayward lover who had finally come back home.

She'd started not to go home. Times were changing, and why should she honor a woman who, for all of her life, had denied her own mother's existence, when all of June's friends were beginning to display their ten-inch Afros and dark, dark skin with a brazen pride? When Black Power and raised fists had replaced heads bowed in shame, how could she understand her grandmother's continued rejection of her Native American blood, and her adoption of the white man's, as a way to explain hair straight as a waterfall and skin the color of whipped honey?

If not for her father's hushed words when he gave her the papers, she would have thrown the envelope in the trash bin on her way to the train station. He told June how his mother— whose illness had brought her to her son and daughter-in-law's home for those final four months—had painstakingly written out a story told to her in her youth about her own mother. Recorded it for a young girl about to begin her own journey. And how two weeks before his mother took her last breath, she had given her son that story, pleading with him to "give it to Junie, it's all I have left."

And now, with the train's rhythmic movement reminding her that she was a captive audience, caught in that in-between place, June had no choice really but to read what her grandmother had written for her. She looked down at the first page, mouthed the title of the story, *"Hija de la Luna,"* and gave herself over to it.

There was no moon. The only sound was the rustling of clothing as they made their way in the black of night like a stubborn wind. Despite the darkness, there was no fear of losing oneself on the way to the Great Tree. Theirs was an ancient knowing, a knowledge of a path that had been traveled for over two thousand years, and even if no one had ever gone before them, the old blood would have remembered the way.

"Mother Moon is hiding tonight." Rosita's disembodied voice floated from somewhere near Viandra's right shoulder. "It seems she is teasing us."

Viandra's thoughts were elsewhere, and so she could only offer the other girl a muffled response. Rosita didn't seem to notice her friend's preoccupation as she rambled on, undeterred.

"All I've heard since you got back is how good you've been doing at school. Your mother's been 'just happening' to drop in on everybody in the village to brag about her daughter. My parents don't miss the opportunity to remind me that I am doing nothing with my life. Does she know you are going tonight?"

"We haven't had a chance to talk much since I've been home."

"Well, she really is very proud of you, you know."

Viandra didn't want to think about her mother tonight. For her, the other woman's pride only emphasized her own hidden feelings of betrayal and honor and shame, feelings she wasn't sure she could tell apart anymore. Instead, she pulled her wrap around her face, gripping the cloth in her fisted hand to keep the wind from snatching it off her head.

The wind at night was different from the breezes at day, she knew. Breezes are playful, filled with the mischief and cleverness of children. It is not until Father Sun retires, leaving the reigning of the earth to his wife, Mother Moon, that what was once an innocent frolic becomes something akin to wicked.

Night was the time when shape-changers and lost spirits roamed the earth. But it was also the time when the Zapotec, Mixtec, and Pueblo peoples appeased Mother Moon with their Great Tree ceremony. Viandra was not afraid of a moonless night. She was Zapotec Indian, and though this was her first time at the Tree, she had already heard the old stories. She had grown up at the cook fires of her grandmother, listening to the tales of the Ancients.

"You are Zapotec, Viandra," her grandmother would tell her in the old language. "You are not like the Mixtec or half-breed, even still outsiders. Yours is the blood of the first people to walk upon the earth."

"Tell me about them, Ba-Ba—the Ancestors."

The old woman squatted at the fire, her deeply lined face

softened by its glow. She was one of the rug makers who sat in the *zocaló*, the central plaza, of a town surrounded by mountains on every side. She was the one with silver hair plaited into two thick braids that hung on either side of her head at the point of her ears. She was tiny, wizened, overlooked by many of the tourists who bought her homespun wares. But to the Indian people she was a woman of powerful medicine, a keeper of the knowledge. She was one who could still speak the old tongue, one of the few in all of the villages who taught the old ways. Even when the first missionaries had begun to consume the land and it became dangerous to cling to the old ways, the old woman had refused to let go. Many whispered that she was a shape-changer herself, or even *la Hija de la Luna,* the Daughter of the Moon.

A toothless grin split the crevices that were her earthen face. "The Ancestors. Let me see."

"Stop teasing, Ba-Ba. You have forgotten nothing."

"You think?"

"Yes. Tell me, please, Ba-Ba."

"All right, sit." She patted the only empty space on the cooking mat, the rest covered with bowls of ingredients for that evening's meal. "Great Spirit created Father Sun and Mother Moon, who were not yet parents to the Zapotec, for they had never had the opportunity to see each other. While Father Sun ruled the earth, Mother Moon slept, and while Mother Moon ruled, Father Sun slept. Well, one day Mother Moon decided to wait up and discover who this other was that reigned in her absence. In the skies she hovered, cloaked in the pinkish hues of dawn, as Father Sun rode his horse to where she sat. When he saw the beauty of her, the silver of her countenance, the long ebony hair that streamed down around her, its tendrils snaking throughout the heavens, he was enthralled. And she, too, fell in love with the handsome warrior astride his white stallion, a vision of strength and power. Of course, everyone knows what happened next."

The old woman stood up and stretched towards the ceiling to gather a few of the blood-red peppers that hung there. She then stooped over her wooden board, took her stone, and began to crush the handful of peppers in silence. A pungent scent soon filled the room.

"Finish, Ba-Ba."

"Oh, yes. They built an adobe, Father Sun and Mother Moon, and lived together for many years, until Mother Moon began to swell with children. She gave birth to her first children, who were the first nation of Zapotec. But the children died almost immediately."

"What happened to them, those poor babies?"

"Well, you see, there was no sun in the skies at day nor moon in the heavens at night, for the two were so much in love that they could not bear to part for even a moment. So the children could not live on the earth. Mother Moon grieved until she was again with children. Yet each time she gave birth, those ones, too, died. And again and again she grieved. One day she decided to travel to the temple of Great Spirit to plead for his help. It took her thirty days to reach him, and when she saw Great Spirit, she cried out for him to assist her. Great Spirit took pity on Mother Moon and answered her pleas. He told her what to do, saying that once she was with children, she and Father Sun would have to part. Father Sun must protect the children for half of the day, and Mother Moon nurture them the other half. 'But I will never see my love,' she sobbed. Great Spirit again took pity and agreed to help her and Father Sun. He told her that he would allow her and her husband to come together, but only twice a year, and for only a few moments each time."

"But why?"

"Because whenever the two lovers are together, they forget about everything but each other. The earth suffers. Darkness descends over the land and stays there until they resume their positions in the heavens. With the lights of the skies no longer protecting and nurturing them, the earth and the people of the earth could not live. When Mother Moon realized Great Spirit could do no more, she began her travels home. Her heart was so heavy that she could eat nothing during her thirty-day journey. By the time she reached her destination, Mother Moon had grown so thin and weak Father Sun feared she would die. Father Sun distilled the maguey plant to make a powerful medicine and nursed his wife back to health. When she was well enough, he lay with her. Not long afterwards, Mother Moon discovered that she was full with children once more. She told her husband what Great Spirit had said. Father Sun was grieved so that he pulled his braids and ripped his garments. He ran from their dwelling and danced his mourning dance until he was too spent to rise. Finally he came to his wife and told her that he would wait until the children were born, and then he would go."

"Did he go, Ba-Ba? How could he leave her, his true love?"

The old woman tossed some thin strips of lamb onto the cast iron skillet. The meat sizzled as it struck the heated metal, the light-pink flesh turning a golden brown.

"He had to. In order for their children to live, Father Sun and Mother Moon had to care for them. They could not be together as before. After the children were born, Father Sun and Mother Moon went their separate ways. They called their children the Zapotec, children of the gods. The nation of children thrived and walked upon the earth. They grew in number so that some had to spread into other lands. All was well, but with only meeting her husband twice a year, Mother Moon grew lonely for her love. She threatened to leave her place and go to her husband forever."

"Is that why we honor her, to keep her from feeling lonely?"

"Yes. But we must always thank Mother Moon, too, for the great sacrifice she has made for us. And so she will never leave her place in the sky. Now run, let me finish my dinner."

Viandra glanced up into the sky, wondering if tonight was the night Mother Moon had decided to leave her children and join her husband, Father Sun. She shivered.

"Are you frightened, Viandra?" Rosita asked.

"No. I have put off this day for too long to be afraid. And you, Rosita?"

The girl lowered her voice to a hoarse whisper and leaned into Viandra. "I am struck with terror, really." She grabbed Viandra's free hand into both of her own. The two continued on in near silence, the leather of their sandals sliding across the pebbled ground the only sound.

After several moments Viandra spoke. "Do you know the legend of the Great Tree, Rosita?"

"I know some of it—most of it, really, but my parents are like your mother, though not quite as bad. They, too, have tried to forget much of the old ways."

"Na, I know. My mother did not teach me. She cannot teach me what she looks at in shame." Viandra looked in the direction of her friend. "Let me see if I can remember it all. There is a legend about when the Ancestors settled this land. It is said the Zapotec increased so quickly that they soon outgrew their homeland. Some decided they would leave and search the earth for a new land. The only thing they took with them was a sapling grown from the Relic Tree, the cypress that had been planted in honor of Great Spirit, Father Sun, and Mother Moon. When they came to the land of Mexico, though it was not yet called by that name, the earth was covered with mountains, and the people were tired. They fell down exhausted and prayed to Great Spirit to show them where to build their home. Great Spirit led the people to make camp at the base of a mountain near a field of the maguey. He taught them how to distill the plant and make the mezcal, how to use it for the ceremonies."

"I know the mezcal is used in the Great Tree ceremony."

"More than used; it is the only way to have the visions. It is the same powerful medicine once given by Father Sun to Mother Moon to nurse her back to health." Viandra searched the heavens.

"Did you forget the rest?" Rosita asked.

"I am only now realizing how much I cannot forget." The darkness hid the wry smile that flirted over Viandra's lips. "That night, after setting up camp and making mezcal, the Zapotec had their first Great Tree ceremony. The ceremony was for Mother Moon and the people both. As Mother Moon pines for Father Sun, she grows weak, thin. The ceremony restores her. In gratitude, Mother Moon bestows visions, strength, and power on her children. So they planted the tree in the center of the camp in the barrenness of the sand, and danced around shouting and beating their drums.

"This continued for days. Afterwards the people saw that the sapling had grown to the size of the old Relic Tree. One warrior had a great vision from Mother Moon. She showed him a mighty place on top of the mountain by which they were camped. The warrior told his people about the vision, and they cut down the top of the mountain until it was completely leveled. They built their beautiful temples and pyramids there, and their ball courts. It took over four hundred years to complete, but when it was done, it was a testament to the gods. They called it Monte Alban. And to this day the Great Tree and the Indian people have dwelt at its foot."

"That is a good legend, Viandra, a proud one." Rosita looked at her friend. "Ba-Ba?" she whispered.

"Yes, my grandmother. She told me all of the old stories."

"I remember when she went to join Great Spirit. I was eleven—twelve?"

"Ten. We were in our eleventh year."

Shortly before she died, Viandra's grandmother called her granddaughter to her bed: "Come, Viandra. There is yet another story for Ba-Ba to tell you."

Viandra scurried across the room and jumped into her grandmother's arms, pulling the blankets around her. Ba-Ba rubbed Viandra's legs to take away any chill as the girl snuggled into the crook of her grandmother's arm, letting the soft, cool skin caress her cheek.

"Tell me your story, Ba-Ba."

"They are your stories, too, Viandra. More yours now than mine, *niña*—little one. Now, there is in every generation a powerful woman. She is a type of medicine woman, but much more special even than that. She is called *la Hija de la Luna*, the Daugh—"

"Ma-Ma, I have pleaded with you to stop telling Viandra these tales." Viandra's mother, Lucerna, stood in the doorway, one hand on her full hip and the other scratching at the thin gold cross that hung around her neck. She walked to the center of the room. "I don't want my child hearing this foolishness. She's too young, too impressionable."

"What too young? Look at you, Lucerna. I told you these same stories when you were her age—younger—and still you no longer remember the ways of your people. You are a white woman now."

Lucerna's face darkened. "That's ridiculous. I will always be Zapotec, as much Indian as you. I only choose what is best for Viandra and me. You, on the other hand—you don't know what you are doing to her."

" 'Doing'?" The old woman gathered her granddaughter to her sagging, withered breast.

Lucerna continued, ignoring her mother's interruption. "You are the one who's hurting her. You will see. In the long run you will be the one who has hurt her most. She needs more than this."

"Like what you have, perhaps? Teaching from the white man, work that forces you up before Father Sun can even reach his place in the skies, chained to Man's idea of time. You are a slave."

"So you say, old woman. But what will Viandra do when she is hungry and finds she cannot eat your legends?"

The two stared into each other's faces, each seeing something in the other's that made her want to turn and run. Finally the old woman took a deep sigh and lay back against her mat. "Good night, daughter."

The next day Viandra's grandmother was too busy to finish the story from the night before, almost purposely so. It wasn't until late that night, when they were sitting on the ground in front of their home, that the two were able to talk.

"Viandra, you must always hold to the secrets of the Zapotec. So much, I know, but seek Great Spirit, Mother Moon."

"I'll let you teach me, Ba-Ba."

"No. Your mother was right. Never leave to others to teach you all that you must know. That is a slave. You will never be that. Now go inside and get ready for bed."

"I want to stay with you. I will stay with you forever." The child grabbed her grandmother's arm in both of her small hands.

"Let go." The old woman pushed her granddaughter away. "I am tired."

Viandra moved on unsure feet as she made her way to the room she shared with her Ba-Ba. She prepared herself for bed and a sleep that did not come easily, haunted as it was by dreams.

The next morning, the child found her grandmother's body sitting outside, where her spirit had left it sometime during the night.

Everyone was still. They had reached the foot of the mountain, the Great Tree. The people, as if on cue, began to form a circle around the base of the ancient cypress. As they parted, Viandra caught her first glimpse of the Tree prepared for the ceremony. Lit torches had been stuck into the ground, also forming a circle around the Tree. Flickering flames danced in the wind, throwing strange figures against the twisted bark. In some places the Tree's skin resembled that of a wild buffalo.

Rosita stood on Viandra's right, and a young Indian boy on her left; the others were mere shadows, their faces hidden in the black. "Ija-waaa," someone yelled out, startling Rosita. Viandra tightened her hold on the other girl's hand as they sat down on the cold, hard ground. Viandra's wrap had fallen unawares around her shoulders, and her long, coal-black hair, whipped up by the wind, lashed across her face. The boy handed Viandra the bowl he had just taken a drink from. Viandra clasped it in both hands. She could smell the mezcal as she raised the bowl to her mouth and drew a deep swallow before passing it on to Rosita. Liquid fire filled her mouth, rolled down her throat into her belly. Another fire, a slow, thick heat, emanated from the center of her womanness and spread throughout the rest of her body.

Someone on the other side of the Tree, unseen by Viandra, begin the steady beat on the drum, until she believed the languid, methodical rhythm came from within herself. The pace quickened, reaching a frenzied pitch as those around her began to whirl in dance. Viandra, too, could feel herself rise up from the ground. She heard someone call out to her in a tongue even more ancient than the old language, yet somehow she understood every word: "Viandra, *niña,* come up here."

Suddenly she found herself at the very bottom of the mountain; everything else around her had faded. The swollen moon burst through the night sky with a silver incandescence. Viandra looked up to find that a thin stream of light had cut a path into the side of the mountain. She began to climb, oblivious to the sharp stones pushing into her bare feet, the wind that shook her slight frame.

Viandra reached the top of Monte Alban. Its ruins, long-abandoned missionary churches that had been built atop the Zapotec temples, now appeared to her, like ghosts rising from the bones of a people.

"Viandra." The voice came from both inside and outside her, an unearthly echo. "Don't you know who I am, daughter?"

Viandra admitted that she did not know who spoke, and with that realization, shame flooded her. She thought of the passing years and how she had learned to despise the sheen of her hair, the darkness of her skin, the blood that claimed her as anything other than white.

The dream she had had the night of her grandmother's death came rushing back to her. But this time, instead of a girl-child of ten, she was a woman who stood on the mountain. She was sitting beside the cook fire making large circles on the floor with her finger. A large snowy owl entered the room, its wingspan filling the entire space. She tried to grab it, but each time she did, it swooped just out of her reach. After several long moments the owl flew out of the house and into the sunlit sky. Viandra stepped outside to find the bird circling just over her head, as if waiting for her. Then it flew away. Viandra broke into a run, chasing after the owl as it went faster and faster until it was nothing more than a dot on the inside of her eyelids. She was left standing in a field of flowers far from the village, far from everything she had ever known.

"No," Viandra screamed, looking up at the moon. "No. Don't leave me again. I need you, Ba-Ba. Please don't go."

She fell down in the lush field and drew her head to her knees. "You left me. You left me." Viandra's balled fist struck the ground. She rolled over onto her back, both arms stretched out, spread-eagled. "I left you," she whispered, hot tears streaming down her face. She watched as the heavens began to pulsate, spiraling into a myriad of colors. She reached out her hand to touch each one as the rainbow pressed itself against her.

First she felt the emerald, heard the color as it dissolved into her, filled her with images: thick, verdant fields, the warm glow of burning cook fires, the scent of venison drifting on cool breezes.

Sienna: mountainous earth slowly rising with each step. Deep moans sweeping the air.

Amber: sun-bathed stone, the velvet whispers of young lovers.

Red: smashed skulls. Surging rivers of blood and the stink of carcasses.

Viandra absorbed the colors one by one, searing into herself the history of a people, until only one color remained. It was a color Viandra had never seen, or perhaps it was the amalgamation of all colors. It was the color of hope, at moments rolling shadows of deep purple and the intense purity of billowing white. She touched it, and the image of a small girl kneeling in a field of flowers with tears spilling from her eyes overwhelmed her. Viandra opened eyes she had not realized were closed. The colors vanished. She pushed herself over onto her knees and saw that the field was filled with white-necked ravens, the band of feathers a badge of honor around their necks, the contrast between black and white accentuating the bird's graceful beauty. Viandra raised her arms above her head.

"*Despiértense*—wake up."

Startled, the birds swarmed upward, blotting out the sun, blackening the sky.

The moonlight streamed through the darkness as Viandra got to her feet. She heard the voice that was her own speaking. "Your name is Strong Winds, Vientes Fuertes, Opke Uwa. In every tongue it means the same. You turn the spark into flames. You are what makes the bird fly, carrying the raven forever upward."

By the time Viandra reached the bottom of the mountain, the sun had started its trek across the heavens, painting the land an array of golden yellows and burnt orange, the sky a dusty pink. The people had started to prepare themselves for the journey back to town. Sleeping forms littered the ground around the Tree. Silently, Viandra strode to the place where her sandals and wrap lay. She plucked them up, gathered them into her arms, and turned to go. As she made her way back to town, she could hear the whispers of those behind her.

"Shape-changer," one said.

"Daughter of the Moon."

Breathless, June looked up from the pile of papers, now strewn across the seat next to her. She pressed her forehead against the window and stared into the distance. The sun had set, and she noticed how quickly the darkness came now. But every few minutes the light would come through, and she would catch a glimpse of her reflection in the glass, a lone young girl with lips a little too thin, a nose a touch longer than it ought to be, and each time she was shaken by the sadness she saw in the eyes that stared back at her.

A VERY CLOSE
CONSPIRACY

Hiron Fuller lived like a man used to being tricked, the way he moved through the world as if intruding on the space he occupied, every step hesitant and afraid. And in the early breath of dawn, that was how Hiron crept from the sleeping farmhouse to make his way to where Walter P. waited.

The smell of damp hay met him as he pushed open the door and entered the crimson barn.

"Mornin', Walter P.," he whispered into the darkness.

The mule, who was just finishing his morning meal—a meal left over from the night before—lifted his head and watched as the only master he had ever known came over to his stall to set him free. Silently, the two left the barn and headed down the shadowed driveway and onto the dirt road that led them in the direction of Moss Woods. Once they had reached the road, Hiron raised his eyes to the distant line of trees that stood like fallen angels caught in the ebbing moon tide. Their branches were flung wide in desperation toward a Heaven they had once called home. And it was toward this the man and his swaybacked companion now traveled.

Hiron had come to enjoy the forty-minute walk to the Richards place, a trip he had been making daily each way for a little over a week, though it meant he had to leave his bed in the early hours of the morning and did not make it back home until well after sundown. Lord knew Ma'D was happy. She wouldn't care if he had to walk to Timbuktu and back in order to get work, Hiron thought as he left the road to cut across the field that stretched beyond the orchards.

The surrounding area had been tilled recently, exposing the black soil that lay beneath, filling the air with the scent of moist earth. Small furrows ran parallel to where he and Walter P. trod, as if the fingertips of some significant Being had caressed the softened ground, marking the direction he needed to go. Between the sense of that unearthly presence and the scent that hung in the air, Hiron grew heady as he approached the cluster of trees and the ever-increasing twitter of birds that seemed to announce his arrival into their world.

Hiron released a breath so deep it surprised him. He felt safe in the thickness of these familiar trees, the way the ground swallowed each footfall and silenced his passage. Here Hiron could escape Ma'D's cold gaze, Hira's empty, searching look, and Cinny's accusing, terrible stare. Not to mention the faces of Tavi and Cease, his youngest daughters, who, thank God, were not yet old enough to put together any real understanding of their father. Hidden like this from the folks who saw him as the town drunk, Hiron could almost forget everything that reminded him of what he could not give, or be, or undo. Deeds unspoken but never forgotten. Here, even the dark thing that came to him at night, the thing that sounded like the rustle of bat wings, was silenced. Not even the drink could do that.

The sun had begun to peek through the foliage. Hiron could tell it was going to be another hot one, like yesterday.

"Too hot for this time of year," he worried aloud. "Things is gettin' crazy, Walter P., anytime Motha Nature can't make up her own mind."

Hiron looked around at the skeletal trees, winter's death cloak apparent in their meager leaves. He glanced down at his feet, where wildflowers appeared in full bloom, subdued of color, tender shoots deceived into believing it was already summer. With each step he became aware of an unseen battle, each season fighting to take her rightful place on the earth, and the realization nagged at him like a hungry, persistent mosquito.

He shook his head, tightened his grip on Walter P.'s rope, and tried not to think about anything except the work he had to do once he reached the Richards place. The rest of the trees that had to be cut down, the stumps that needed to be pulled up from the roots, so Mr. Richards could do what any "decent" father should: build his daughter and her new husband a home of their own. And he had come to Hiron for help.

Hiron grinned to himself at the idea of a white man hiring him to do such an important job when no one else in town would offer him a nickel to carry a sack of groceries. He didn't realize that the only reason Mr. Richards hired him in the first place was because he could get by with paying Hiron half of what he'd have to pay anyone else. But Hiron was down to another week at the most and then he'd be done. Unless he could persuade Richards to keep him on, he would go back to being what Ma'D called a shiftless no-account.

Ma'D. Hiron didn't know what he was going to do that evening. It was Friday, and she would be expecting him to hand over his pay. The thought made him pull at his lower lip with his small, even teeth. He wondered how he would tell her about the advance he'd taken. How he'd spent it on drink. He wouldn't even have to say on what—hell, she'd know anyway.

"I can just see her, Walter P."

Her lips would clamp so tight they'd disappear. And the look she'd give him, the coldness of it. Hiron hated the way she could make him feel without even opening her mouth to say a word. Just the thought of going home made him shudder. He felt Walter P.'s weight pull against the rope in his calloused hand, and he looked back over his shoulder, watched as the mule raised his face to the smell of sweet grass on a stray breeze, his nostrils quivering. Hiron raised his own face, closed his eyes, inhaled deeply.

He tugged on Walter P.'s tether. "Come on here, boy."

I know what that's like, Hiron thought. Like when he'd first met his wife. When just the smell of her was enough. He could still see her as she was then, when she was Dorothy Mae. Sixteen and running behind a mess of siblings. Young and so alive.

He had just received word that his father was dying, laying in that house of his, alone and in pain. His liver worn down from years of rot-gut bootleg. Hiron had come down from the city to say his good-byes, prove to his father that he could be a man and make amends. The two never had gotten along, even though Hiron was an only child, and a son at that. His mother had run off when he was still a baby, leaving father and son to make some type of a life built on blame and mutual suspicion.

Even still, he had come. Planned to stay until his father was gone before returning to the life he had made for himself in the city. But for Ma'D.

A smile creased Hiron's face as he remembered walking along another dusty road in the heat of the day. Watching from a distance as she chased down her wayward sister. How she'd darted past him like a honeybee, throwing a quick "Hey" in his direction. Tripping over just what, he never did see. And him lunging forward to draw her work-hardened body into his own. He could still see her dust-covered ankles and feet, the sweat-dampened tendrils of hair that curled on her forehead, the eyes that laughed at him and made him smile. And the smell of her! Like sun-baked cornfields. To a man who had become used to city fumes, she smelled like down home.

And so Hiron had lingered. For the days and weeks it took his father to die. And then long after his father was dead and buried, and the will was read, and he discovered that the old man had sold everything to one of the neighbors. Even after he had been somehow diminished in the eyes of everyone in Grandville, when it would have been far easier for him to go, Hiron stayed. Never had gone back to the city. All for a woman-child still young enough to believe in fairies and magic and a man like him. A woman who, by just the scent of her, could make a man feel like he had finally made his way back home.

"Home," Hiron snorted, turning back to look at Walter P. "And now I'm skeered to death to even go near the woman!" He laughed, a laugh that sounded more like a man choking to death, and then fell silent. Continued his trek through the thickest of trees.

Hiron wasn't sure of the exact time. He didn't own a watch, though he had always dreamed of having one—a gold pocket watch with a matching gold chain that would hang from the top of his waist. Like the ones the older men in town carried; like his father's. Instead he could tell the day's unfolding by the sun's unfailing passage overhead. He and Walter P. would reach the clearing in another twenty minutes or so. The Richards farm was yet another two miles after that. A good enough distance away from that young couple, Hiron thought. Not like when he and Ma'D got married, while the country was at war. Two weeks later the words of the white army recruiter, about how this war would be the one to change the plight of the colored man in America, found their place in Hiron's heart, and then he found *himself* on a ship, heading for a country whose name he had only read in schoolbooks. A people whose language he didn't even know.

Back then, war had meant promise, of Hiron finally becoming the man he knew he could be. Matching what he saw when he stood in front of his mother-in-law's full-length mirror with his uniform on, his chest swelled until the buttons strained. He wished his father was still alive to see his son the soldier. Going to the front line to defend his country's freedom against the Japs and Germans. The idea filled Hiron, sustained him through the humiliation of basic training—where the officers refused to give the colored men anything other than fake wooden guns—and lasted until well after he had reached the other side of the world. It lasted until he learned that each of his requests for special training had been denied and he became the personal driver to one of the white officers. Hiron realized he would spend his days behind the wheel of a government car, or opening the door of a government car, or cleaning a government car, instead of fighting in the purity of a battle for liberty.

And the nights, they were spent in acute aloneness, a condition he hadn't felt since he was three years old and realized he was a little boy whose mother had left him while he was yet a suckling. Even when Hiron played poker or shot craps with the boys, or hung out at one of the French clubs, he felt as if there was something that separated him from those around him. But it was when he was stretched across his bunk, writing Ma'D letters filled with stories of heroism stolen from the lips of others, that Hiron felt most obscure.

For months he lived like this, like a man standing at the edge of time. Waiting for something, anything. Papers that would transfer him into the real war, make the words written on pieces of paper somehow true. But before anything could happen, the war was over. And Hiron found himself on yet another ship, this one heading for home.

He could still feel the moment his feet had touched American soil, when he stood on the dock in New York City, surrounded by people who all seemed to know one another. Women hugged their husbands' necks, and mothers clung to men, once baby boys who had clung to their breasts. And all Hiron could think of was getting back to Ma'D.

He had picked up his duffel bag, slung it over his back, and stridden down the street to catch the bus that would take him to the train station. Without thinking, he fell in behind a group of white soldiers, fixing his eyes on eight feet covered in the black mirrors of patent leather, the hems of khaki uniforms still crisp despite their long journeys.

The details had burned themselves into Hiron's senses. The black rubber-treaded stairs when the bus pulled to the curb and the door opened with a long, slow hiss. The cold railing against the skin of his hand, grown soft over the past ten months. The dime in his other hand, slick with sweat, its metallic, bloodlike smell. Hiron could still see the driver's doughy face, the bulbous red nose that separated an ice-blue stare.

He could hear the clink of the metal as the coin slipped from the tips of his fingers and slid into the collection box. Could hear the words as he started down the aisle, words that sliced through his skin and found their place in that part of him that was kept hidden.

"Where the hell you think you goin', boy?"

Hiron had stopped dead, his feet pinned to the floor by the faces of the good white folks sitting nearby, their eyes grazing past him as he pulled his head, turtlelike, into his shoulders, before bowing and scraping back down the steps and out the door. He felt something deep inside begin to shrink with each step towards the back of the bus, where he entered through a different door, his eyes desperate, and searched the gathering of black faces, only to be met by the immobility of seemingly spiritless expressions. But for the anger he found in each sidled stare. The way they looked at him as if he was to blame.

He had thrown himself into the first available space, though it meant having to squeeze himself beside a woman whose hips took up both her own seat and half of the one he occupied. He wanted to disappear. Closed his eyes and tried to think about Grandville. Going back to a place where he wasn't even the man of his own house. And Hiron knew in that instant what it felt like to exist and not exist, all at the same time. And the knowledge frightened him.

That was when the nightmares had started, and he could no longer find the man he used to be in Ma'D's eyes. And when he understood that he might have to live the rest of his life like that, from an angle instead of head-on, the only thing to comfort him was the drink.

"Well, there's one thin' I got from the war, Walter P. Taught me how to hold my liquor. How to drink lak a man." Hiron laughed again, then sighed. "I must be gettin' old, boy. Goin' on, dredgin' up bones."

Hiron emerged through the trees marking the edge of Moss Woods, swatted at the branches that brushed the side of his face as he stepped into the clearing. The sight stopped him short as it did every morning, filled him with awe at its consecrated beauty. The grass shone emerald green, the dew creating a sparkling web that stretched unbroken for miles and glinted like a net of diamonds in the morning sun. As much as he hated to disturb this place, Hiron unloosed Walter P. and made his way to where he'd left off working the day before, leaving a trail of broken dewdrops that collected like tears across the toes of his boots.

Hiron's ax lay wedged into the top of one of the stumps. He reached over to retrieve it. When he first started this job, Mr. Richards had tried to persuade him to use the power saw on the trees, but that seemed more like a violation than anything else. For Hiron there was something about the feel of the ax's smooth handle in his hands that made him feel more connected. Who needed all that newfangled stuff anyway? He grabbed the ax handle and worked it up and down until it pulled free from the wood. Without hesitation, Hiron went over to the remaining clump of trees and struck the first blow. The first tree's outer bark was stronger than it appeared; it would take several strokes before he could embed the ax blade into its pulpy flesh. While he worked, Hiron talked to himself in the guise of Walter P., who had wandered to the nearest patch of grass and now paid Hiron no mind.

"People always wantin' stuff, Walter P. Just more junk to get rid of when you die, 's all." The ax hit the trunk once more with a loud thud.

"Power saws and such. Like television. Everybody goin' crazy over a picture box; radio's not good enough no more. Nuthin' good enough anymore." Hiron fell silent, though his thoughts continued to flow unchecked.

He could feel the fullness of the day as it completely replaced the dawn. The stirring of insects and animals, the very air around him wakening until it hummed with a vibrancy that had been absent just a short time ago. Everything seemed different under the sun's glare. Where before the dawn had settled melancholy in Hiron's belly, the increasing light seemed to set him on edge, made him feel much too exposed. Like the blade of his ax as it sliced through the space around him, slipping into the innermost part of each tree.

After the war, nothing had seemed the same. Ma'D had gone to work in the factory, like most of the other womenfolk who wanted to eat while their men were away. The knowledge that she could do the same job as any man made it impossible for Ma'D to go back to where she'd been, and made it unlikely that a man like Hiron would be able to settle back into his old place. Not knowing what else to do, he stayed out late, drinking and gambling with the other soldiers who had made it back from the war.

But with Ma'D and his mother-in-law always fussing and picking at everything he did, those nights became more of an escape. Them and Ma'D's younger sister. The way that

twelve-year-old looked at him, her eyes wet with adoration—
like Ma'D had once looked at him herself.

He could feel his stomach clench at the memory of his
wife's baby sister. He didn't want to think about her. A grown
woman now, who had moved away from him, away from
Grandville, as soon as she was old enough to do so.

But then he'd found out that his wife was pregnant. And
Hiron was given another chance. He'd passed out cheap ci-
gars bought at the whistle stop even before Ma'D began to
show. Swaggered around for weeks on the idea of being a father to a baby he was sure would be a son. A boy he would
teach to hunt and fish and throw a baseball.

He had lived on that dream for six months, until Ma'D
gave birth to their child, a girl-child named after him, Hira
Juniper Fuller, binding him to the sickly blue thing. She reminded Hiron of a baby mouse, the way her skin folded and
sagged around her, all covered in soft, furlike down.

Hiron's ax bit into the tree, his swing hard and sure.

From the very beginning Hira had been demanding, stick-
ing her claws into Hiron with her colicky cries that pulled
him from his sleep each night. He refused to touch the puny
creature, which didn't bother Ma'D or her mother: Hira was
theirs, and they made sure he knew it. But there were times
when his gaze would rest upon his daughter's sleeping form,
and the desire to take her in his arms with such tenderness and
the wish to crush the life out of her would rise in him. The
sight of her, her eyes closed slits, her mouth opened and seek-
ing, would fill him with such disdain as to leave him weak and
shaken.

Hiron checked the ax's swing in midair as the tree began its slow descent toward the forest floor. He brought his hands down by his sides. His chest heaved with both exertion and fear. He had worked up a sweat, and he took a few moments to unbutton his denim work shirt, pull it off his arms, and toss it onto the ground behind him. He looked around for Walter P. and spotted the mule off in the distance, sniffing and licking at whatever caught his attention, with an animal's curiosity, just a whistle call away. Hiron thought to summon the animal to him but decided against it.

I'll just leave him be.

Hiron retrieved his ax and began to cut away at the last section of bark connecting the fallen tree to its base. He would wait until day's end before having Walter P. drag the felled trees into a pile. Mr. Richards would take them to the lumber yard, where the bark would be stripped off and nature's once-majestic creations reduced to mere slabs of boards and piles of dust.

Hiron moved over to the next tree and swung his ax from behind his shoulder with a powerful blow.

Wasn't a whole year after Hira's birth that Hiron's mother-in-law was gone. Seven months later his father-in-law, a kind but silent man, suffered a heart attack in his sleep and went to join his wife. Folks say whenever there's a death, a birth's not far behind, and four months after they buried her father, Ma'D found out she was once again with child. As the months went by, Hiron tried to become what Ma'D needed, relieved that he was finally free of his in-laws, that relief in turn filling him with guilt. And at times he grew convinced that his mother-in-law's spirit had taken over his young daughter, the way Hira's chestnut eyes followed him around the room as if she was waiting for him to do something wrong. There were times when Hiron was sure he could see the old woman hiding behind his daughter's eyes. Especially when he stumbled home in the dark of night, and one of those vicious fights started that were supposed to be between him and Ma'D, and he'd happen to glance up to the top of the stairs and see his daughter hunched in the corner, and that other one lurking behind, peering at him from the shadows.

Hiron shuddered despite the sweat that ran down the center of his back. He wiped the rivulets of water from his brow before getting back to work.

He could tell that his second child was special from the moment she entered this world from the one she'd once occupied. The midwife told the story of his daughter's birth all around town—how that child never uttered a sound, just looked around the room with ancient eyes, sucking on the hand she'd stuck into her mouth, like she was taking inventory of this world and realized she already had everything she needed.

Cynthia Mae Fuller had been pink and healthy from the first, already filling out skin that would darken quickly over the next few months. Unlike Hira, she hardly ever cried, having figured out it wouldn't do her much good anyway. Hiron could hold her without fear, and he did. Sat in his wife's rocking chair in the evenings instead of going out with his swinging buddies, talking to his daughter until his words became a steady hum and she fell asleep in his arms. Cinny was his, just as Hira belonged to his wife. It was him Cinny crawled for, him she took her first steps for. Raising each leg as if she was a marionette on someone's string. The toothless smile that stretched across her boneless face once she'd realized her father was no longer holding on. Hiron absorbed each one of those memories into himself. The feel of her skin. The smell of her.

The second tree cracked as it pulled away from its base, startling Hiron, pulling him from thoughts of his daughter. He watched as it, too, fell to the ground. Without even stopping to take a break, he went right to the next tree and began to attack its bark with the ax that had by now become an extension of his hands. He struck again, the steel ripping deep into the tree's V-shaped wound and exposing the untouched flesh inside.

But Ma'D couldn't stand to see him contented. The things she'd said to him when she was angry. The ugly accusations about his true feelings for the little girl he held to his chest. Reminding him of his sister-in-law, who had moved on by then. How he'd spent his time with her, meeting in places he thought were hidden from the ever-watchful, ever-disapproving gazes of Ma'D and her mother. Ma'D's words chased him from the house each night. And then Tavi and Cease, and with them the realization that he would never have his son. When the truth of their existence had been reduced to Ma'D's keeping a roof over their heads and their bellies full. It was like falling. And for him there was only the drink, and then Cinny.

Hiron's head began to throb with things he didn't want to remember, things that came to him at night and haunted his dreams.

It was Ma'D's fault. She was the one put those thoughts

about Cinny in his head. Made it easy for his love to turn into something he could no longer control.

The ax whistled as it sliced through the air. The steel caught the edge of the tree with a glancing blow before sliding easily into Hiron's leg, just below the knee. His right hand was pulled free from the force as the ax anchored itself into his flesh and knocked him off balance.

A scream tore from Hiron's throat. Without thinking, he yanked the ax away and grabbed at his leg with both hands. Blood flowed through his fingers, bathing them in its warm stickiness.

Hiron moaned, panted.

He fell down to the ground, squeezing his leg with all his strength. He tried to quiet himself, tried to keep from panicking. Hiron turned to look for both Walter P. and the shirt he had just removed. Walter P. was just where Hiron had last seen him, the shirt a few feet away from where he now sat. Without taking his hands from his wounded leg, Hiron scooted himself over to where his shirt lay. Quickly he snatched it from the ground and wrapped it around his thigh, twisting the arms into a tight knot to press against the vein. The blood slowed to a trickle. Where at first there had been very little pain, the leg now began to throb to the beat of Hiron's heart. He could feel the bile rise into his throat. He closed his eyes and opened his mouth, swallowed large gulps of air to keep from getting sick.

He had to think.

Hiron scooted over to the stump of the tree he had just cut down, rested his back against the rough bark. He had to figure out what to do. He could call Walter P. and have the mule take him to Mr. Richards's place. Wasn't far. He'd have enough time to get there and get help, as long as someone was home.

Mrs. Richards. He continued to tell himself to breathe—slow, even breaths. She'd be there, and she'd help. And Cinny could take care of him once he got home. Cinny had been taking care of him for a long time now. She was a giver. The one who had climbed onto his lap and told him stories with him as the hero and her as the princess. Hiron bit at his lip, pulled at the skin until it bled. And he had taken those stories, every one of them.

He remembered how his mother-in-law used to say that Ma'D was taken with him. It had been a long time since anyone was taken with him. Looked at him with the same wonder and awe with which he had stared at that field this morning. Everyone should be looked at that way. As if just the sight of him caused the breath to catch in the back of the other's throat. Cinny had once looked at him that way. She had made him believe. Hiron's head fell backward against the stump. His leg ached. He opened his eyes and stared into the liquid sky and asked God what he had done.

The woods seemed to grow suddenly still as Hiron tried to ease the fear that threatened to take him over. Thoughts rushed at him that he was just too weak to keep at bay. He thought about Ma'D, her sister, Hira and Cinny. His girls, who once, like him, had believed in princes and princesses. Who knew about monsters. But not Tavi and Cease.

Not yet.

Hiron looked down at his leg. His denim work pants were soaked through with blood. Without giving himself time to reconsider, he unwrapped the makeshift tourniquet and pulled the shirt away to expose his wound, and immediately the blood began to flow from his leg and seep onto the ground.

His monsters: his father and the white man, the war, and then Ma'D herself. All he'd ever wanted to be was a man.

Hiron coughed, the movement sending waves of pain throughout his weakening body.

Dying right now, like this, he knew they'd all say it was the drink, but he also knew that in a few short years his name would be the stuff of legends. Hiron Jackson Fuller, the one who died a man. And Ma'D would be the widow, no longer the wife, of the town drunk. And Cinny and Hira would finally have their hero.

"I'm so tired," Hiron mumbled to Walter P., who had come closer to where his master struggled.

Hiron's eyes began to fall shut as his head fell forward onto his chest. Darkness rushed up to meet him there, and he was reminded of his dreams. He jerked himself awake, tried to struggle to his feet. A gasping panic swept away all of his resolve as he grabbed at the shirt that lay rumpled beneath his leg and tried to rewrap it.

"I'm scared, Walter P." His hands fell by his side, his chest pounding with fear.

Walter P. looked at him with a concentrated gaze, his almond eyes filled with something akin to pity as Hiron fought to hold on to the last vestiges of life.

"God help me! You've got to!" It had been a long time since he asked anything of a God he wasn't even sure existed.

He looked back up at the sky, the topmost branches of the trees. And for a moment the scattering of leaves became hands reaching up, across, dipping down to where he lay. The sight brought tears to his eyes, tears that fell unchecked down his dusty face. Hiron felt a calm enter him, like a woman being loved by a real man. He could feel the terror dissipate as it left his body. He knew he was taken care of, had always been, and that knowledge convicted him. As the stillness of the universe settled into him, Hiron realized that this was the moment he had lived for. Every day struggling, and it was this moment that meant something.

Hiron's gaze took in everything around him: the trees and sky and Walter P., who stared at him with large, brown eyes filled with unwavering acceptance. And it was enough.

Hiron laughed when he thought of how close he had come to playing a part in his own demise.

AT THE WATER'S END

He'd thought the poet dead, or at least silenced. But as he stood at the edge of the porch watching his father, words flooded his head and rained down at his feet.

Dixon Bentlow was slumped over the wheel of his boat, a vessel he had owned for as long as Scoogie could remember, though it had never left the front yard. Instead the *Bentlow* sat on a rusty trailer that had long ago become a nesting place for rabbits and raccoons and any other animal in need of a place to call home in a field of overgrown weeds. And every day Scoogie's father manned his "baby," empty beer bottles and a fifth of hooch littering the area just around his boots, a sailor's dream taking him off on another one of his drunken adventures.

"Dammit." He turned and entered the farmhouse, letting the door slam shut behind him, and stepped into what his mama called the front room. The dimly lit house appeased him, with its familiar figurines and whatnots, the heavy oak sideboard and china closet polished to a high shine. He could see his mother's touch in everything around him, and he felt his anger slip into a mild irritation as he made his way to the kitchen.

His father had always dreamed of becoming a man of the sea, though all of the Bentlow men had been farmers. He blamed his desire on the Mysteries, his name for the nameless ancestors, the ones who had first crossed the ocean and stirred up the restlessness that would pass through the generations. His father's dream had become a chain around the poet's neck.

He could smell his mama's supper, cabbage and turkey wings, welcoming him even before he entered the room; his empty stomach acknowledged the greeting. Working the fields made a person hungry like that, made it so all that mattered was the body's most basic needs. He figured that was the reason his father could hardly stand to go to the fields anymore: he knew a man could lose his dreams out there.

Scoogie waited at the threshold, leaned against the wall and watched while his mother prepared her family's meal. She went to stand in front of the potbellied stove, her hands fluttering from place to place, stirring and mixing,

Like birds drunk with the sweet taste of flight.

And he realized he had never seen his mother still, her hands at peace. And she talked all the time and much too loud. Even if conversing with herself, she spoke so that anyone could hear, her words always a step too late, a heart rhythm just off beat, waiting for someone to respond to the complaint of a headache, or a cold, or any of the other illnesses that had become her only protection against the brutality of her life.

Sad, isn't it?

"Hey, Ma," he mumbled, fighting to ignore the poet's commentary on his mother's existence.

"Hey, Scooge." She turned with a smile on her face. The bruise cupping her left eye drew his gaze. It was a nasty yellowish green, garish against her soft, ginger-colored skin. "Where's your father?"

"You mean the Cap'n, don'tcha?" He pushed himself away from the wall and sauntered over to where she stood.

She turned her attention back to her pots without responding to the challenge in his words.

"And where else would the greatest Cap'n in the whole world be but at the wheel of his impressive ship?"

"Scoogie, please."

"Please what?"

When she didn't answer, he pulled himself to his full height so that he towered over her, his voice raised. "Please what?"

She spun to face him, shrinking from the unrecognizable image of her son with clenched fists and a hate-darkened face. "Scoogie?" She placed her hands on his cheeks. "Son," she whispered.

Scoogie lowered his head at the gentleness in his mother's voice. His shoulders sagged as the anger drained from his body and he went back to looking like the young boy she was used to.

"He stayed in the boat again, Mama." His voice shook like a child's. "I missed another day of school."

"Oh, Scoogie, I'm so sorry." His mother gathered him into her arms. "You must be tired and hungry, huh?"

"Yes, ma'am, I'm real tired."

"Go on and wash up, then. By the time you done, your supper'll be on the table."

"Yes, ma'am." He stepped away from his mother and wiped at his eyes.

"There's my sweet boy."

Scoogie looked around to make sure his father hadn't come into the room and heard his mother call him that. "Don't say that," he hissed, moving over to the other side of the kitchen to put some distance between himself and his mother. "You know what he thinks about stuff like that."

He could still hear his father's words, questioning his manhood, calling him a fairy and a queer. And especially when he found out Scoogie's desire to become a poet. But the poet had fought back. Spoken the words of freedom and escape, kept him hungry for something other than what his mother could provide. Until the day his father found the notebook, took it to the backyard, and burned it. Killed the poet. Or at least that was what Scoogie had thought.

"Your father's a damned fool, is what. And don't you pay him no mind. You hear me?"

"That's near-'bout impossible." He shook his head and grabbed the banister with his right hand, his left bracing the wall. "Don't matter noway. The fields are making sure of that."

He watched his mother struggling to say something, words he was sure would be too small for what he was going through. She shook her head as he disappeared into the stairwell. He was dead tired, a deep, wrenching, muscle-aching kind of weariness that made him feel much older than his sixteen years.

Scoogie headed straight for the bathroom and shut himself inside. It was cool in there, almost cold, because of the tile and porcelain and the window so small that hardly any sunlight came through. It was just what he needed, he thought as he sat down on the edge of the tub with his head in his hands.

Guilt filled him. He felt sorry for the way he had just spoken to his mother. He loved her.

Hatred wears love's mask,

He shook his head. He loved her and maybe pitied her. But he could never hate her.

and they both appear the same.

No! Scoogie jumped up from his seat and reached for the cold-water tap. He'd been so hateful lately, everything stoked in him a burning rage, and it frightened him.

Scoogie peered into the mirror that hung over the sink, searching his image, though for what, he wasn't quite sure. When he was a little boy, he'd had to be mean, had to fight almost every day. All the children taunting him about matters they couldn't possibly understand, the gossip their parents traded over shared cups of coffee or glasses of lemonade, like they were discussing the weather or what Mrs. Mason had worn to church last Sunday, instead of the screams that came from the Bentlow house to break the stillness of the night air.

And then he'd somehow gotten past all that.

Living with what the soul knows should never take place.

Like that mess with Pontella. God, he hadn't thought about that in a year.

Scoogie stuffed the stopper into the drain and turned on the faucet. He wished he could ram something down the poet's throat. He watched the bowl fill with water, wondered what the old gang was doing. Junie and Sonny had been the first to break away, and though he saw all of them every day, it wasn't the same. They didn't know one another anymore. Not like when the six of them swam naked in the creek and swapped blood from the smallest of scratches and swore to a brotherhood that would last for the rest of their lives.

But they'd never really known him, either. Never known about the poems that sang in his spirit. Even then he was afraid.

Scoogie heard his sister calling for him to come down and eat. He splashed his face with the cool water until he felt revived.

His father and youngest sister were already seated at the table, while his sister Emily, who came just after him in age, helped his mother serve the food. Scoogie took his place at his father's right and unfolded his napkin. He could smell the whiskey on his father's breath, and it sickened him.

Only after everyone else had been taken care of did his mother and sister sit down with the rest of them. If not for his mother's insistence, his father would have started the meal without a hint of a prayer. But even he had enough sense to thank God for His provision. Scoogie closed his eyes. It was hard seeing a man like his father utter words that ought to be sacred.

They didn't talk at the table. There was something about sharing a meal, having to face one another, that made it too easy for a word or a look to set off a war. Instead they ate in a tense, fearful silence.

Scoogie looked around at what remained of his family, his parents and his sisters Emily and Alexandra—meek, pasty-looking girls whose spirits had already been crushed by the only love their father knew how to give. His other two sisters had already married and moved away with the first men who showed any interest in them. They called to check on their mother but never came to visit the ones who hadn't yet made it out. He missed them. Didn't realize how much he would until they were gone and it was left to him to take care of everyone else. Though he had often tormented his younger sisters, he had also tried to protect them and his mother. Had made it his job to do so, even if it meant throwing himself in front of a fist flying too fast and too hard to stop. But tonight, seeing the three of them work at chewing their food quietly so as not to disturb his father, he felt as if he had somehow failed them.

He looked at his father, who was smacking his lips and sucking his turkey bones as if he had never eaten before, and made every attempt to hide the disgust he felt inside. "Daddy?"

"Whassit?"

"The fence in the back field needs fixing."

"So fix it, dammit." He stopped eating long enough to give his son a look of frustration. "You s'posed to be a man now. I shouldn't have to tell you that." He pointed his fork at Scoogie. "If you was on the water and you saw a problem with the boat, the Cap'n would expect you to handle it."

"I'm not at sea, sir."

"But you was raised a seaman. And you know better."

"Yes, sir."

"Good. I expect you to take care of it. By tomorrow." His father tapped his fork against the table. "Zeta, fix me a slice of bread." He could barely keep his eyes open.

Scoogie watched as his mother started to get up from her seat even though the basket of bread and the butter dish sat right in front of her husband's plate.

"Why can't you fix it yourself?" Scoogie blurted.

" 'Cause she's my wife and that's her job. The lazy, good-for-nothin' bish."

"Don't talk about her like that."

"Scooge—" His mother stretched out her hand toward him.

"Don't you talk to me like that, sailor!" His father reared back in his chair, nearly knocking it over. "Now, I said fix me a slice of bread, goddamn you!"

"And if she don't?" Scoogie's voice was quiet, daring.

"Scoogie!" his mother screamed at him. "Please, Scoogie. Don't do this to me."

"To you? How can you say that?"

She rushed over to his father, who sat in his chair as if it were a throne, his head bobbing all around as if his neck was broken. Before his mother could get a chance to do anything, Scoogie grabbed her tiny wrists in his hand. He squeezed hard, causing her to yell out from the pain.

"I said, fix me a piece of . . . ," his father murmured, saliva trickling from the corner of his mouth.

"Don't do it," Scoogie hissed.

"Let me go, boy." She began to struggle, but he just held on even tighter. He smiled.

This is what it feels like.

Shut up! He flung his mother's hand from him and watched as she carefully slathered a piece of bread with whipped butter, just the way his father liked it. She set the slice on the side of his plate and went back and sat down at her place across from him.

As soon as she picked up her fork, his sisters, who looked as if they had been afraid to swallow, began to chew whatever was stuck in their jaws, and all three of them tried to ignore the snores that came from their father and husband's open mouth.

He kept his eyes on his mother. He felt betrayed, alone. She had never been there for him, he thought.

*And how could she be, when she was so busy trying to
save herself?*

Just like now, he figured. She chose.

As if seeing her for the first time, Scoogie looked at his
mother, who ignored him. The poet had always been there
for him. His comforter. Had whispered to him when he'd
been forced to run, to hide in the back of the closet beneath a
pile of clothes, or under the bed amid the dust and cobwebs.

Fear can kill you, you know.

The poet had said that to him one particularly cruel
night when the sound of his father's work boots striking his
mother's skull had chased him into one of his hiding places.
The poet had even been there on those other nights, usually a
few days after a beating, when the sounds that came from his
parents' bedroom made him believe he would go insane. The
moans that tore from his mother's throat possessed a rawness
and a heat that terrified him more than any of the other
screams, that shook the earth from beneath his feet and spun
it off its axis until he no longer understood anything. And he
now knew that each time his mother had tucked him in and
promised that she would take him and his sisters to a place
where they could all be free, she'd been lying.

He looked back and forth between his mother and father.
It was all a part of the dance.

And the music is madness, and pain.

And fear. But he was tired of being afraid, scared to stay, terrified to go. He didn't want to dance anymore. Didn't have it in him. He loved his mother. And hated her. He'd always thought his father was the only one, but the emptiness consumed them both—all of them, really. The abuser and the ones abused, not really opposites but

Reflections of the same hollow soul.

As long as his mother could look into that mirror and find herself reflected there, she would stay. Until the images changed, she would stay. And he grew scared, aware that both of them could be found inside him, too. He knew what he had to do: he had to be the one to choose.

He jumped up from the table and grabbed the box of matches from beside the stove and ran out the door. He ran around to the side of the house and grabbed the can of kerosene his father kept there. It was the boat, he thought as he stumbled through the dark. It had never been the poet, only the boat that was the problem, he told himself. By the time he reached the other side of the yard, he was desperate. He flung the can of kerosene so that the liquid splattered in all directions, drenching the boat, the hem of his pants, his denim shirt. The waist-high grass so heavy it leaned almost flat to the ground.

His chest heaved, the fumes and the fear making it so he could hardly breathe.

Will you kill it?

"What?"

Like you tried to kill me?

"I didn't kill you, *he* did."

Did he?

Scoogie hesitated. "Yes, it was him, the Cap'n."

Do it, then.

He didn't know what to do as he stood there bathed in moonlight, feeling as unguarded as when he was a child. When he'd waited, breathless and eager, for the world to tell him everything about himself. Before he'd needed someone like the poet.

And just as he was about to make up his mind, he saw the night sky begin to split its belly wide, opening itself to what could have been the rising or the setting of the sun—he had no idea which—to reveal cotton-white sand and the bluest, clearest water he had even seen, so vast its end seemed to touch the sun's surface. His father's boat stood forlorn at the water's edge. And again he felt anger at its sight, struggling to replace the bone-deep wonder and awe that the sea inspired in him.

The world is terrible.
The world is beautiful.
It is.

He walked over to the edge of the pool, the water licking at his feet, and leaned forward until he caught sight of his own reflection. And he saw that the image was weeping, each tear flowing down and mingling with the ocean, rippling outward, reaching for what he decided had to be the sun at peace. There was no choice to make anymore and every choice to be made. He knew why the sea was as clear as dewdrops in the hush of dawn: it was made up of his tears, joy's and pain's.

And the sufferer's tears are the purest.

LIKE DOVE WINGS

I remember when she come back home, carryin' her blues in a faded pink blanket, edges frayed. I was the first to see her. Half stumblin' down the road. In the darkness. My own restlessness makin' it so I couldn't sleep. Even from where I sat, I could see a bone-weariness all over that poor child, the way her arms held on to that baby only because they been used to doin' so. I thought about how we all be holdin' on, even if what we holdin' on to is a whole lot of nuthin'. How we go through life pretendin' to be full up on emptiness.

I used to believe the only thing worse than leaving this place was having to come back in need. But life has a way of making your worst fears greater than the point it brings you to, until nothing else matters except putting one foot in front of the other, in front of the other, in order to find your way back home. Even still, I come back to Grandville at night, a shame that is not my own keeping me from treading the street in broad daylight and under the eyes of those who once created the me I used to be.

She wouldn't come out for the first three months she was home. Didn't want nobody to know about a baby with no father and a young girl whose dreams amounted to a faded blanket and a half-mile trek back down a dust-covered road. But I knew. Just like I'd known she would leave in the first place. Could tell she was the runnin' kind.

When she finally decided to show herself, it was at church, of all places. That baby on her hip. Struttin' down the aisle to the pew her sister, Loretta, usually took every Sunday. The sight of Ebbie, her citified self, caused a heat to rise in the already warm room. Womenfolk fanned themselves, ashamed for a girl who didn't have sense enough to be ashamed of herself.

As soon as I knocked on the door, as soon as Loretta answered, I knew what I was in for. Her eyes, tight at the corners, accusing, greeted me in silence. When she helped me into a chair so I could rest my feet, and took Pontella from my arms, it was with an unforgiving face. And if my own sister, my flesh and blood, could look at me as if she didn't know who or what I was, I could only imagine how the rest of the town folks must feel about me.

So I stayed close to the house. Never left except at night, when Pontella was down for the evening and the only thing looking at me as if I had some explaining to do was the frogs and crickets, creatures whose world I had disturbed when they thought they were free to sing.

❦

She ain't come back to church after that first time, though we see her around town every now and again. Time passes, and I can't explain it, but I find myself lookin' for her. Thinkin' about her, wonderin'. While Dorothy, Irma, and Zeta chitter like a bunch of squirrels, gossipin', I stare off into the distance, tryin' to wrap my mind around what this woman was and not what they say she is. They say she some kind of a witch. Say they men been actin' real funny ever since she come back. Folks arguin' more 'n usual. The chirrun carryin' on like they don't have a lick a sense. And it's been near 'bout a whole year and ain't nobody got pregnant. Whispers say she done somethin' to dry up our wombs. Done stole our seed.

❦

I can't go back to that place. The way everyone's eyes read my life from the rips in my clothes and the baby who slept in my arms. It was as if they all thought they knew everything they needed to know about a woman like me. And when the coldness filmed each gaze and hardened every familiar face, I knew I would never find in them what it was I needed.

154

Funny, but me sitting in church, in the house of the Lord, was just like that woman in the Bible, the adulteress, and every single one of those God-fearing church folk were ready with stones. Except Jesus didn't come and gather me up. He didn't shield me with his body or stoop down and write something in the dirt at my feet. I knew that if I were to continue to go there, all I would do was keep them from taking the planks out of their own eyes, because they'd be so busy tending to the stick in mine.

※※※

Yesterday the weather broke. There is a hint of prefrost in the wind, causin' my cheeks to redden when I'm outdoors too long. Folks will be stayin' in more. Ebbie, too. Though she ain't out much anyways. Gone are the days of watermelon chillin' in the icy creek until one of the men strikes it against a rock to split it open. The sweet flesh explodin' on the tongue.

But the hog'll be delivered soon, and it'll be slaughterin' time. A season for killin'. It will come innocent, unawares of its fate. Squealin' in its pen in the back of Mr. Kenton's truck. And after a few days, Leonard will slit its throat from ear to ear. String it up by its back legs to drain the blood. It will become cuts of meat: a ham shank, slabs of bacon, its bladder a balloon to be tossed about. And me and Leonard will feed on it all winter long, forgettin' the day it come to us in the back of Kenton's truck. Whole.

※※※

Fall comes quickly, bringing with it cool days and even cooler nights. I watch as the earth and the things of the earth prepare to bed down for winter, hoping that I, too, will be able to settle in. Like Pontella has done. How she runs from room to room like they all belong to her. The way she tastes and touches everything that catches her eye and that's just within her reach, as if by feasting on balls of dust that scurry across the floor and dead spiders hidden in corners, she'll become one with this world.

For a squirrel, say, or a two-year-old without memory, finding a place in the world is an easy thing to do. But for one who has never known her place, a woman's place, it is nearly impossible. So I stumble through green kitchen, into white bedroom, and back through blue parlor, trying to catch sight of something—anything—that resembles me, just to keep from falling away.

❧

Somethin's been pullin' me from sleep almost every night lately. We got the Indian summer and the nights are warm, even though the leaves have already started to change in their eagerness for somethin' different. I go to sit on the back porch, my mama's shawl wrapped tight around me like arms tryin' to hold me together, and even there I feel the pull to go down to the Pinder place, just to see if she's still there. Just to get a look at her.

Everybody sittin' around talkin' about her like she a dog, when all she did was what half of us have wanted to do at one time or another but was too damned sorry or scared to try. Too busy worryin' about what everybody else'd think. But nobody'd admit it. Then they'd have to say that maybe somethin' was wrong with all of us, too. Instead, me and the others make like Ebbie's the one need fixin'. At least that's what we say out loud.

⁂

If not for my baby girl and the night, I would die here. Each day I play with Pontella little games I've made up. I contort my face into silly pictures that make even me giggle. Or chase her around the yard until we both fall exhausted, laughing, on beds of grass. The smell of her skin and hair after I have given her a bath, me nibbling at the layers of pudge on her legs and arms, around her neck—I drown in the scent of all that innocence. But that's what keeps me during the day.

At night I creep outside to sit beneath the moonlit sky. It's there I get what I couldn't get in church that Sunday. At those moments I know I still belong to this world, this universe. Just like the trees and the earth and the stars. I find something out here that even Pontella can't give me. Out here I don't have to be a child's mother, Loretta's sister, or that Pinder girl who ran away. Out here, with God looking down on me, where their shame can't follow me, I'm just like His other creations. Only I'm a tree whose roots have pulled free, a sunflower that no longer follows the movements of the sun.

⁂

And when I couldn't stand it no longer, I went down there. To the Pinder place. I saw her sittin' in the backyard under a cluster of trees a little ways from the house. She held her face to the moon like she was at church. I wanted to go over to her and hold her like I would a child, amazed by how small she looked under the largeness of the sooty sky. I expected her to be six foot tall by now. Like she should have grown from all the signifyin'. How big we had been makin' her with our words. In our own minds. But she was small. I wondered how we all must look when we got to stand alone. How I must look on the other side of the road, hidden in darkness.

❧

I saw that woman Leonard married standing across the street, watching me. At first I was angry. I figured she must have heard I was the one he'd once loved, though we loved in secret. A woman knows. She can always tell when there has been another, can feel the presence of another like a shadow that hovers just out of reach, blocking out the fullness of the sun, causing a chill that goes down to the bones. And then I felt sorry for her: the one who comes to see the one who loved a man she can never know. A man who strolled among whispering trees and still dreamed dreams. As if by seeing me she might somehow discover what it is she wants to see in him.

❧

Before I could call up enough sense to stop myself, I ran down the road and over to where I knew she'd be. My mouth opened and the words spilled out of me like one of those angry rains. They was hard and fast, the words that spewed from me:

158

Who you think you is comin' back here like you some movie star? With no shame whatsoever. How dare you? And now our chirrun actin' up. Our husbands. Stealin' our seeds, makin' it so all we can talk about or think about is Miss Ebbie Pinder, hauntin' me so's I can't even sleep at night—why you have to come back here remindin' us of what we done tried so hard to forget?

When I was done, I fell to my knees in the grass beside her, my chest heavin', too empty to cry. My words had been the tears, and the prayers, my mournin' song, and in the tellin', they had become hers, too.

❧

When I looked up, she was already standing over me as if she wanted to strike me. Her hands were clenched in fists so tight they shook. Even in the moonlight, her eyes looked like pools of glittering black glass. I sat, too stunned to move, while her words fell over me and pierced my skin in accusation, until I realized she wasn't talking about me at all. Then I watched as her words became snow that tumbled from her trembling lips onto the grass and dissolved into the earth, feeding the rich brown soil while the air between us grew heavy with pain and loneliness and fear. When she was done, all I could do was lay my hand on her bowed head and whisper over and over, "I know, I know."

❧

Now we meet almost every night, meander through the orchards in silence. Or sit and talk. Mostly we talk, comment on how two women so different could be so much alike, inside where eyes don't go. How one could leave this place, the other one stay put. And we realize the reasons were the same: fear. One afraid she would turn out like everyone else, the other scared to death she wouldn't.

We share secrets denied us in our youths. The truth about who we are. The stuff no one wanted us to know. We share the story about the women called maniacs. Women who lived a long time ago. They were just country women, really, who got tired of cookin' and cleanin', takin' care of the husband and chirrun. Got tired of everybody else usin' up what was supposed to be their lives. So they met in the woods one night and had this dance. When the men found out, they got angry and tried to put an end to their women's foolishness. But they couldn't. The women rebelled. Started gatherin' every night. Before long the men started callin' the women crazy, and started treatin' them like they was, until the women began to believe it.

Why is it when a man wants to be free, he's just being a man, but when a woman wants to live life from the position of the birds, the first thing folks say is that she's crazy?

That's what we ask ourselves.

We shake our heads as if unsure of the answer. But we know. It's because they know what'll happen if we ever really do get free. They scared.

❧

Ebbie say God must be a woman. That we was made in Her image, though she whispers it like she's afraid He may hear her talkin' about Him thataway. I tell her she's blasphemin'. Ebbie say she been blasphemed against all her life. That I been blasphemed against, too. Just because we womenfolk. She asked me to think over how many times someone spoke to me, to my womanness, with irreverence. Me. A sacred bein' like them stars, only Ebbie say more so 'cause I was fashioned in God's likeness. And me not ever knowin' it. I laugh at her, but that night when I creep back home and let myself in the screen door, real quiet so's not to wake Leonard, somethin' deep down in my belly tingles at the idea of God with Her nappy hair, coffee-and-cream skin, and lips thick as plums. Lookin' like me.

❧

Ruthie craves a child of her own the same way I once ached to leave Grandville. So I tell her about when I was pregnant with Pontella, when she first fluttered. And the women who already had children—how they told me it would feel like I had a belly full of butterflies. Only it wasn't like that at all. I'd felt butterflies before; they came with the fear.

This was something else. More like dove wings, bringing me peace for the first time in my life. And for a while I thought I was having a bird, until I saw the coal-black coils of hair peeking out from between my thighs. When the midwife turned Pontella's head in order to sweep her mouth, seeing her face, that ancient face, I realized for the first time that a whole being had lived in me. The awe made it so I could barely breathe or move.

I could hardly hear the midwife telling me to push one

more time, the shoulders. And me taking the deepest breath I could, so deep my chest burned, hunching my back and pushing with all of my might. I felt in my soul more than in my body the ripping, like the ripping of the veil. Shaking, I fell backward onto the bed, my eyes rolled up into my head. It was like I'd fallen into the bluest of oceans, sinking, sinking into the warm, rushing waters of life. I had fallen into myself. I had become the world, my womb the center of the universe. I had become one with God, one who knew what it meant to be creator. Life-giver.

That's how I know God is a woman.

Ebbie gives me permission. That's all, permission. Like someone sayin' it's all right to just be. And whatever all I was meant to be in the first place. Before they told me that girls couldn't chew gum or climb trees or wear jeans. That a woman's value counted on how well she fed her husband and children and the way she kept up her home. Before they told me a girl-child was what you wanted only after findin' out you couldn't have anythin' at all. I believed 'em, every one of those bald-faced lies. And them some powerful lies, too, anytime they can talk a person out of bein' what God made her to be. Talk a person right out of her soul. But Ebbie come along and tell me the truth of the matter. Truth always burn away anything that ain't like it.

Selfishly, I tell Ebbie that I could go on like this forever. As soon as I say it, I see somethin' in her eyes shrink from my words. At that moment, I know it's only a matter of time before she leaves again. I tell her how it gets harder for me to fit myself into a life that someone else created for me. Never understood that it wasn't even supposed to be thataway. And when I leave her, I'm scared and angry all at the same time. Scared to think of what I have to go back to if she ever leaves me, angry at the ones who made it so.

Tired of bein' treated like a fall hog.

Ruthie comes to me after two days, her eyes hidden, black ice cupped by purple moons. I look at her bruised face with both anger and guilt. Someone else's desecration making me feel responsible, and her ashamed of her womanhood, her vulnerability. She says Leonard beat her because she refused to cook and clean. I don't tell her he beat her because she stopped making him believe that he was the only reason she ever existed at all. Like the husbands of the maniacs, he knows that the young girl he married is already a memory.

When we go to leave the orchards that night, a chill invading the air, disturbing the illusion given by our Indian summer, I know I have to go. For a brief moment it's been enough to know that someone else is as I am. To find myself in someone else. So I won't have to feel so very alone. But I'm the one who made it that way, forcing my own nature on her and maybe even on Pontella if I were to stay.

I say it's getting too cold for us to meet. I promise I'll see her in the spring. I hold her close, inhale the nutty scent of wet earth from her hair, holding back the pain of unshed tears in my chest, knowing it will be the last time. Winter will come and I will settle in with the child I created, make memories of my own.

Ruthie talks about forever as if there really is such a thing. When even our future is already our past. But for a time our souls met, and danced, and soared. We were able to live like the maniacs, and we were comforted by that knowledge.

❧

It's not until spring I learn Ebbie has left me and Pontella. Left before I could tell her she gave me back my seed. Now I walk through my life like one who goes by a familiar place that has been torn to rubble, one who can't quite remember what once stood.

I feel the months slide by and I watch my skin stretch taut over the swell of promise. I could almost pretend like this never happened at all, except for the movement in my belly, like dove wings, remindin' me of my nights with Ebbie and what it felt like to be really free, pullin' me from Leonard's side each night. I sleep beneath maples cast in shadows, lettin' tears fall warm and without excuse. Folks talk so, but to Leonard's face they tell him it's my bein' pregnant. That I'll return to normal once I have the baby. While every night I lie on a bed of grass-covered earth, fall into a sleep filled with dreams more real than this world, where I am a fish the color of rainbows, a bird that soars to the depths of the ocean. They say when a woman is full with life, she dreams strange dreams.

FIC
LINCOLN

Lincoln, Christine.

Sap rising.

$20.00   09/12/2001

DATE		